Egyptian
Exotica

Egyptian Exotica

A Memoir of Dancing Naked

Rania Zada

Brooklyn, NY

Ig Publishing
178 Clinton Avenue
Brooklyn, NY 11205

www.igpub.com

Library of Congress Cataloging-in-Publication Data

Zada, Rania.
  Egyptian exotica / Rania Zada.
    p. cm.
  ISBN-13: 978-0-9771972-0-0
  ISBN-10: 0-9771972-0-4
  1. Zada, Rania. 2. Stripteasers--United States--Biography. 3.
Egyptians--United
States--Biography. I. Title.
  PN1949.S7Z34 2006
  792.7--dc22

                              2006004181

ISBN-10: 0-9771972-0-4
ISBN-13: 978-0-9771972-0-0

Thanks to Hope Edelman for support and feedback of this project, my husband Greg for his encouragement and faith in me, and my family for giving me a space to write and for just plain putting up with me.

prologue

My father was a jeweler, and as a child I liked nothing better than to watch him set precious gems into rings and necklaces. In his tiny workshop in Egypt, he had a large pale green powder box full of diamonds, rubies, emeralds, and sapphires, all in different shapes and sizes. I used to dig my tiny hands into the box and watch in wonder as my fingers disappeared, buried in the sharp sparkle. I used to ask my father what would happen to me if I ate a mouthful of diamonds. Would my mouth shoot out beams whenever I spoke? He would laugh.

My parents divorced when I was four, and I was raised by my mother and grandmother. Dooya, as everyone called my grandmother (it was a nickname I had given her when I was a child), was a willful and proud Egyptian woman who had no patience with anything or anyone but me. She took care of me while my mother worked long hours to make ends meet for the three of us.

When it came to my mother, I was always in a state of conflict. I wanted to be close to her; I thought she was beautiful and relished the attention men threw at her. (I couldn't wait to grow out of my scrawny figure and develop curves like hers.) However, she was always angry with me, or with the world, and would fly into sudden violent rages over the way I looked, the way I talked—everything I did made her scream, made her brow furrow in disapproval. So I learned to walk a delicate path around her, never knowing what would set her off.

In rare relaxed moments, my mother would put on music and dance with me. Taking my hands in hers, she would guide my feet, keeping me in step with the rhythm. As we moved, she would lose that hard look that could stop my heart in fear, and I would find myself, temporarily, in the presence of a woman I very much wanted to be like.

When I was seven, my mother, grandmother, and I took a trip to Greece. The sweltering summer heat lured us out to a boat on the Mediterranean, where I spent several afternoons basting in the sun, trailing a lazy hand in the warm, tranquil waters. The sea was astonishingly clear and still, an azure mirror, its blue depth contrasted by the stark, whitewashed stone houses clustered along the cliffs at the water's edge.

One night, we had dinner at a dimly lit, crowded restaurant. Men walked by our table, casting appreciative glances in my mother's direction as she smoothed her long, straight auburn hair. She had a complexion like tea with milk, and even after a day of salt and heat, she still turned heads. She acted as though she didn't see these men, or didn't care, but I knew better. Meanwhile, my grandmother glared at my mother's admirers, and I am sure that she would've liked to swat them away with the same napkin she was fanning herself with.

After dinner, my mother took out her compact mirror and reapplied her red lipstick. I stared at her as she did this, moistening my mouth with my tongue as she did. She caught me doing this and gently took hold of my chin, tilted it up, and dabbed a little lipstick on my lips. Then she held the tiny compact to my eyes. In the dim light, my red lips gleamed back brightly.

Feeling like an adult, I slipped away from the table and, smacking my lips and smiling at myself as I passed a full-length mirror, I headed toward the dance floor in the center of the restaurant, where a band played festive Greek music. With eyes closed (it was easier, for a shy child like myself, to let go when people couldn't see me letting go), I walked onto the dance floor, and let go. The thick red lipstick was my center, and from that center I spun, feeling the silver lights from overhead reflecting off my lips as I danced around and around and around.

That night in Greece began my journey into dancing. Until then, I had only danced with my mother, but after that night, I danced all the time. At dinner parties my mother threw, I'd get up in the middle of conversations, put on the music without asking, and start dancing. I danced in restaurants, even if they didn't have dance floors. I danced in shopping centers, in airports, in grocery stores, anywhere there was a crowd.

At times it grabbed hold of me violently, the feeling to just move. I wasn't sure if I was coming apart or coming together by submitting to it. But dancing, being up on a stage in front of people, made me shine. It was like eating a powder box full of diamonds.

one

I walked with difficulty through the perpetually crammed streets of North Beach. Cafés with large, open windows bustled with customers; the typically bold San Francisco afternoon breeze blew. At Cafe Roma, some men at a table argued heatedly in French while they cradled their espressos and cappuccinos and flicked cigarettes on the sidewalk. One man rolled his own cigarette, licking the paper with relish.

I crossed Columbus Street, my backpack bouncing lightly on my spine. The Condor, a sports bar where I had been a cocktail waitress, was on the other side of the street. Steve, the old, brooding English bartender, stood behind the bar making a drink for a customer. I slowed down, hoping to catch his eye through the window, but he was too busy to see me.

I made my way up Broadway to where seedy strip clubs like the Hungry I, Adam and Eve's, the Pink Poodle, and the Lusty Lady lined the block. Music blared from every open door, while barkers, stationed in front of each entrance, announced the good times to be found within:

"No cover to get in, no cover on the girls, either"

"Come in, see another world!"

I walked another block and stopped at a nondescript, single-story building decorated with laminated, framed posters of well-coifed women with long hair whipping around their faces. The place was called Glitterati's, and the sign above the front door said, "San Francisco's Most Upscale Gentlemen's Club." How the word "Upscale" had come to be associated with stripping was a mystery to me.

I entered the dressing room and was immediately lost in a sea of women brushing their hair, glossing their lips, primping, and preening. Laughter and private, girlish conversations wafted through the smoky air, which bubbled over with glistening female bodies and the scent of candy and fruit sprays that came out of bottles shaped like hearts, rubber duckies, and kittens.

As I drowned in the overpowering smells of pear glacé, cookies and cream and strawberry-coconut pie, I eyed the various costumes hanging on the backs of chairs and doors, lying on the ground, or bursting out of bags. Dynamic costumes. Expensive costumes. Epic costumes. These women didn't wear black; they wore dark ink plumes that howled at midnight, a witching hour to be slipped over the skin. No wool, no cotton, nothing ordinary.

My own backpack, light and pitiful, didn't hold such treasures. I looked around the room at the Italian matching luggage, the garment bags, and the duffel bags as big as my own body. All were filled with necessities, the necessities of being a stripper. I'd only been stripping for little more than a month and was determined to be Someone at Glitterati's.

I shoved past everyone, found my spot in front of the mirror, and opened my backpack to take out my makeup, which was wrapped in a plastic grocery bag. I observed my tired face in the mirror for the first time, watching my eyes twitch in sleepless exhaustion; I looked like a hungry ghost.

From the bottom of my bag I unearthed a simple black spandex dress that screamed slut. As I put it on, the surrounding girlish jingle faded until all I could hear was the sound of my own breath.

I was eight years old in Egypt, in a nightclub with my father. It was a humid summer night, smothered in jasmine, and my father smiled past me, eyeing a voluptuous belly dancer bejeweled in red chiffon and golden bangles with strands of sparkling beads strung like ropes over her hips. The tiny cymbals on her fingers clinked hypnotically to the pounding of drums.

My father handed me a strip of paper with his phone number scribbled on it and whispered into my ear. I obediently rose from my chair. I walked to the stage with my legs wobbling, and my eyes burned as the dancer twirled a blood-red shawl around her milky midriff. As I stood beneath her, the drums pounded into me, and I reached up with the piece of paper. Seeing me, she bent down and took the paper from my hands. I didn't let go. She moved closer, until her face was next to mine. Her sleek, dark hair cascaded over her eye and fell in liquid waves over her shoulder.

"F-f-from my father," I heard myself stammer. As instructed,

Egyptian Exotica

I kissed her cheek gently and was immediately engulfed by the scents of lipstick and musk mingled with the faint salt of her sweat. I squeezed my eyes shut and felt her twirl the shawl over my shoulders and head, covering my face. When I opened my eyes, I saw the audience springing to their feet, applauding and swooning and hollering. I nearly toppled over.

At age twenty-two in San Francisco, I rummaged through the lost-and-found box, trying to find the threads of someone else's lost magic to wear, instead finding nothing.

I got up and squeezed past a few women to get to one of the full-length mirrors. I stepped around duffel bags and scattered high heels and mumbled "excuse me" to a couple of women sitting on the floor, applying coats of nail polish to their toes, giggling about something. The dressing room at Glitterati's was always like a girls' slumber party. When I finally found a mirror, I stared hard at myself and tried to ignore the greased, sinuous bodies writhing in the reflection.

"You've gotta cover up your tattoos," someone remarked behind me.

I turned around; her face was oval and tan, offset by deep green eyes and dark lashes. Her straight, thick brown hair was swept over a shoulder and fell over oiled, tanned breasts and dark pink nipples. I cast my eyes down, then quickly looked back up to her face, not wanting to seem like I was checking out her nipples.

"But it comes right off," I complained. The manager had told me that tattoos needed to be covered up, but the makeup caked off easily. My tattoos are small, anyway, one discreetly located on the back of my shoulder, one at the top, and another in the shape of a small eye on my right shoulder.

"It's a pain in the ass, but we've got to do it." She threw me a tube of beige makeup. "It's better than foundation. You can get it at the drugstore."

I dabbed some on my shoulder and blended it in, then walked upstairs to the club.

Glitterati's main interior was plush and creamy, with burgundy velvet and candlelight glowing from the booths and linen-lined tables. I walked past the mahogany bar, my heels clacking on the hardwood floors as I touched each bar stool. I had a constant fear of slipping and falling on my face, so I always tried to walk carefully and slowly while also trying to be graceful and smooth. Working in extremely high heels was more difficult than I'd expected. I'd worn heels before, but never for six hours straight, and I'd never had to dance in them.

The elevated stage was backed by a wall of mirrors, and pink lights shone down brightly from above. When the deejay announced my name—"Here is Layla" (my stage name)—I stepped up to the platform and looked out into the club, where a few men watched expectantly. I started to sway to the music, moving faster than I wanted to because I was still nervous about how I looked. Relax, just relax. Just breathe, I repeated to myself. Then, disappointedly, I watched my reflection chug along mechanically in response.

Glitterati's upscale atmosphere catered exclusively to businessmen who were mostly, in a word, loaded. A strictly enforced dress code kept out undesirables: Men had to be dressed in a button-down shirt and sports jacket, which wasn't a problem since most of them showed up right after work.

The strict dress code applied to the dancers, as well. Dresses had to go past the knees; the longer the better. Cute skimpy outfits were reserved for the stage shows, but the floor rules of the club demanded that the women be fit for an invitation to the Oscars.

In addition, music had to be tasteful (no rap or heavy metal, no obscenities in the lyrics, and nothing too weird), tattoos had to be covered up, and every woman had to be polite and courteous toward the customers. While dancing onstage, we had to avoid doing anything too explicitly sexual, such as grabbing our nipples, touching our crotch areas, or inserting our fingers into any orifice —except our mouths, which was considered sexy. Floor work was forbidden, meaning no getting on hands and knees while onstage. Furthermore, when men tipped a dancer, they had to leave the money on the rail and were not allowed to hand it over directly.

"What's all this mean?" I had asked the manager, a Polish woman in her fifties with thick, large glasses and stringy hair, as I signed a piece of paper with "The Rules" written on it the day I was hired.

"For your own good," she had grunted. She had picked her teeth and stared at me. "You sign if you want to work. If you don't sign, you don't work."

Who was she to tell me how to act, what to wear, what to do? For a second, I considered not signing. But then a stubborn determination reared its head within me. I wanted to be Someone.

Rania Zada

I wanted it so bad, I could feel it all the way in the back of my throat, like a cough coming on. I wanted to belong, and nothing was going to get in my way.

I signed.

two

We all stood in a line heading toward the stage. Every two hours we had to do the "lineup," where all the dancers went up onstage together. As we stepped onto the stage, the deejay announced our names and "We Are Family" played in the background. Then, like a chorus line, we sashayed in full costume, dancing, smiling, winking at the stiff crowd, whose formal postures reminded me of obedient schoolboys, their faces lit by the quiet burn of candles.

Nearly twenty of us wantonly gazed into the mirrors on the stage, which took up every corner of the club—a trick to make the place look twice its size. The stage was a maze of mirrors, and to look into one mirror was to look into a hundred mirrors and see a hundred more images of ourselves. The mirrors taught us which angles enticed, which expressions looked best. And which didn't.

Things got a little competitive when we were all up there together. Some of the dancers brushed past me, nudging their way to the head of the stage, their faces full of fierce pride. Because of my passivity, I was always pushed to the back, forced to look out at the writhing bodies. When the song ended, we left the stage to approach whichever men we'd made eye contact with.

I fell behind and sat alone at a table as the club came alive. I watched as champagne bottles were brought out and dancers and customers merged together. The music was thumping, and the mood was like a high-school dance with spiked punch.

A bit apprehensive about the whole mingling thing, I wandered into the VIP room, where, by this time, most of the women had taken their customers for private dances. Ignoring the suspicious glare of a baboonlike bouncer in a suit stationed at the entrance to make sure "nothing funny" went on, I peered inside.

The VIP room was lit with red lights, and red velvet chairs and couches lined the walls for the men to sit on while they got their dances. Small poles graced the four corners of the room. I watched as bikini-clad dancers playfully pranced like fairy-tale forest creatures around their customers, a couple of them grabbing on to the poles, swinging and twirling, striking poses. No touching by customers was allowed; this was strictly a visual tease, set to both spark the imagination and to provide a space for each dancer to work magic out of herself and into her customer. A dance cost twenty-five dollars, ten of which went to the club. In my short time at Glitterati's, I hadn't yet danced for a customer, but from what I'd been told by the manager, as well as from what I'd seen, this was where the real money was made.

A tall dancer with skin the color of silken chocolate and a sleek mane of black hair led a man past me. Her dress clung to her, accentuating every shivering curve of her body.

"Where you taking me?" he asked with a weak smile, which made me think his question really was, What are you going to do to me?

"To the VIP room," she said, smiling, showing off a straight, even set of white teeth.

He surveyed the room warily.

"What's wrong, honey?" she purred. "I thought you said you wanted to be alone with me."

"I do," he said. "But this isn't really what I had in mind, you know?" He gave a little laugh, then glanced at his watch.

"Oh, come on, it's early." She leaned over and whispered something in his ear. He pulled away from her and shook his head.

"Come on," she said, still smiling. "The VIP room ..."

"Listen," he interrupted. "I don't know what to tell you ..."

"Princess," she said as she touched his arm lightly.

"Right. Princess," he smirked, the look on his face turning angry. "Princess, listen to me. I want you and me to be alone. Do you know what the word 'alone' means, honey?"

"We can be alone in the VIP room."

"No, no. Look. I don't want other people around. I want a place where you and I won't be interrupted."

"The VIP room," she said firmly, still smiling. "That's where we can be alone."

"Look, sister. If I just wanted to see you jiggle in your panties, I could've watched you onstage." He walked away, leaving her standing alone with the smile still frozen on her face.

Sensing my presence, Princess turned around slowly, and

I pretended to inspect the leaves of a nearby potted plant. She made her way to another man seated at a table, bent down, and whispered something in his ear. The man shook his head. Princess walked away, head held high, back straight. She saw me watching her again and threw me a sharp look. I went back to admiring the plant's glossy leaves.

In my entire month of dancing, I'd only asked three men for dances and had been rejected all three times. I knew my approach was bad: leaping out from behind various plants and poles, then jumping into a booth with all the subtlety of a Mack truck and startling the men half to death. I was way too nervous to be smooth.

To make things worse, after we were rejected once, it tended to mushroom, as the men in the club watched one another. When a woman danced for one guy, another usually beckoned immediately, having, suddenly, the identical craving.

The stage also freaked me out. When my song started, my ears tuned out every sound in the room, including the music, and my body raced through like every note was a burning room I was trying to escape. I felt like the entire club and everything in it, the glass and the mirrors, were perched on my moving body, precariously balanced; one wrong move would throw it all off and shatter everything. The stage was a sinking ship, and I was the lone captain in the nude, awkwardly steering through a sea of glass.

three

My shift ended at midnight. I walked by the Broadway glare of seedy strip clubs, past a couple dancers hanging out of the doorways, smoking. A man wearing a white undershirt hung out a second-story window and hollered at me with a lecherous little wave, "Hey, Bee-yooti-fool!" I gave him the finger. He laughed. I lit a cigarette and crossed the street to Columbus, then caught a cab to the Volt.

When I lived in Los Angeles, my regular hangout was a hole in Hollywood that didn't have a name. I started going there when I was nineteen, mainly to play pool. The bar was old, with fifty years of yellowed newspapers covering every inch of its walls and a broken jukebox that played Guns N' Roses' *Appetite for Destruction* and some Pink Floyd when kicked at a certain angle. The clientele consisted of aging pool hustlers, sad, old drunks passed out at the bar, and fresh-off-the-bus, cute Midwestern boys trying to make it as L.A. rock stars. Sometimes tall, big-boned, haggard "women" wearing too much makeup and not enough clothing came in to snake their big, manicured hands up the thigh of a rocker's leather pants. I knew they weren't women and wondered if those Midwestern innocents had a clue.

I'd go to the bar in the late afternoon, chat with a few drunks, laugh with a few wannabe rockers, and ask the pool pros for a few pointers. My teacher was an old black man named Downtown, whose wardrobe consisted exclusively of suits from the 1920s. He practiced pool nearly every day with his own pool cue: a sleek, black stick that twisted apart into three pieces, with "D" inscribed at the bottom. As he played and moved around the table, he gripped a thin cigar between his teeth, trailing a cloud of cherry-sweet smoke around his head.

Downtown and the rest of the crowd took me in like a wayward daughter, and for about a year, this was my life. At the time, things weren't good at home: I was fighting like crazy with my mother, who was angry with me for not going to college as decent people did. But I had a fierce independent streak and was driven by strong creative urges, and my urge at the time wasn't to go to college. I instead experimented with writing poetry, doing children's theater, and making money as a movie extra. I plunged headlong into anything vaguely interesting, wanting to consume and be consumed. But no matter what I tried, I wanted more. My entire existence was like a hungry mouth devouring everything in sight, and yet no matter what I did, I remained hungry.

As a result, my mother and I would scream at each other until I would stomp out of the house, get into my car, and drive to that nameless hole in Hollywood. I moved to San Francisco the following year.

Shortly after I arrived in San Francisco, the Volt became my regular hangout. The bar looked like a one-story gutted factory. Heat blasted from the overhead vents to keep out the usual Bay Area evening chill, and PJ Harvey moaned from the jukebox.

It was a Friday night and the busy, smoky bar was filled with new customers as well as the usual array of locals that alternated between the bar and the pool table. The crowd was made up of people mostly in their mid- to late twenties, hip, casually dressed.

I asked Jill, the bartender, for a glass of red wine. Her black dog, notorious for attacking shadows on walls, sniffed at me for a second before running off.

"Knock it off, guys, I don't want her breaking a tooth!" Jill screamed at two guys making shadow puppets on a nearby wall. The dog was jumping up and down, going berserk, butting her head against the surface to try to bite into what she thought was there.

I looked over at the pool table and saw Jack bank the eight ball into the side pocket, then light up a cigarette and shake hands with his opponent, a tattooed hipster. Jack was tall and good-looking, with the best hair I'd ever seen on a guy. He was my friend, and more. Actually, he was just more. He gave me a knowing half-smile when he saw me, as he waited for his next opponent to rack the balls.

Jack began the game by unleashing a series of perfect, effortless shots. His opponent looked pissed off and asked Jack if he planned to let him play any time this century. Jack, too cool to form words, just shrugged. He ran the table and beat the guy without even giving him a chance to play. When Jack went to shake his hand, the guy stormed off with a scowl.

"Fuck this place!" he yelled to his friends, then pointed to Jack. "That guy's a fucking shark!" Jack rolled his eyes.

I lit a cigarette, grabbed a cue, chalked it, and racked the balls. Jack broke, and the table became a stage for us to perform our little ritual. We took turns dancing and twisting while we threw shots, and more, at each other. Jack was by far the better player, but I was pretty good myself, and our pool games had always been fierce. The way a ball whizzed across the table became a dare. When it landed in a pocket, a challenge. When it hit another ball on the way, it was a question, and scratching or missing meant surrender.

With each shot we made, we moved closer to each other, until our legs touched and our eyes locked. The tension attracted other people, who came over to the table to watch us.

"Shark!" someone yelled when I sunk another shot.

"Best to stay out of the water," I replied in my most ladylike voice.

I won that night.

One drink later, I was on the back of Jack's motorcycle, holding on to his waist as we zipped through the foggy streets. I leaned my head against his back, shielding myself from the cold, biting wind.

Inside his apartment, he led me quietly by the hand into his room, not wanting to wake his sleeping roommate. Keeping the lights off, he fumbled around in the dark, trying to find a candle. When he finally found one, he lit it, and pieces of the room appeared, looking dusty in the flickering light. Jack's book collection was stacked in the corner, and piles of laundry littered the floor.

He disappeared for a moment, then came back with a couple glasses of ice water. I drank mine too quickly and it numbed my throat. He took the glass from my hand, put it on the floor by his bed, then slid his arms around me and kissed me on the mouth, removing my jacket and dropping it to the floor as he took a handful of my hair in his fist. My head spun from the wine and cold water, and I grabbed on to his waist, pulling him closer to my body. I struggled with his zipper for a minute, not wanting to yank it down too quickly because Jack rarely wore anything underneath his pants.

Naked, we lay on his futon. I kept my eyes open, watching his face and closed eyes. Even with the candlelight softly blazing, I had the distinct feeling that my desire for him was slipping away. Strangely, Jack's naked body always threw me off. I'd been having sex with him once a week or so for the past year, and every time I touched his body, it was awkward, like it was our first time together.

I leaned over, buried my face into his neck, and inhaled deeply, but as always, he was oddly devoid of any scent, except for faint traces of beer and cigarettes. Distracted, I started looking around the room. He reached over to a little crate by the window, took out a condom, tore at the wrapper with his teeth, and slid his erect penis into it. I crawled around him on my hands and knees, then climbed on top of him.

I closed my eyes and tried to focus, but my mind flashed to Glitterati's, to the stage, to my mirrored reflection staring back at me, bathed in pink lights. I opened my eyes, grabbed Jack, and silently wished he'd put on some music—the silence of the room hung thickly in the air like a watchful spirit.

We couldn't establish a rhythm—our bodies knocked around like a tone-deaf couple at a disco. An hour before, he'd turned me on. An hour before, he'd looked damn good with that pool cue in his hand, a cigarette dangling from the corner of his lips. We were on the back of his bike cutting through dark streets and I wanted to be here. But now I felt nothing.

I lost my virginity when I was sixteen. His name was John, and I met him at a rollerskating rink. We went to separate schools and only saw each other on weekends, but we would talk on the phone every night for hours, until my mother threatened to unplug it if I didn't hang up and get some sleep. When we got together, we would go for long, quiet walks in the mall, holding hands and slipping into corners to gently kiss and grope one another.

He lived in a one-level stucco house that contained many rooms for his many brothers. I think he had five, all of them large and athletic, like he was. His room had a bunk bed that he and his identical twin, Les, shared. Les had the top bunk, John, the bottom, and we used to lay together on his bed and make out for hours, while Les lay above us, reading comics.

After six months of seeing each other on weekends and talking for long hours on the phone and frantically rubbing each other through our clothes, I felt ready for the next step. John gave me a heart-shaped diamond ring and confessed his love for me. It was a sweet, romantic gesture, and I was swooning inside my inner castle of pink clouds.

John's oldest brother, Rick, and his wife, Julie, owned a large house hidden in the mountains outside Los Angeles. The place had a fireplace and heated hardwood floors. We sat in the den downstairs, on a big, floppy red couch, watching satellite television while we held sweaty hands. We could barely look at each other—there was a quiet understanding that this would be our last evening as virgins.

I'd been very protective of my virginity until then. I'd met boys I thought I really liked and had refused to even let them touch my body unless they said they loved me. Most were contemptuous of this caution, and they punished me for it by dumping me off in the middle of a date, onto the street, because I wouldn't have sex with them. As much as this bothered me, I believed I was doing the right thing by waiting until I was ready. The more I was prodded and pushed for sex, the more firmly I dug my heels and refused. I was saving myself for love.

Rick was a good-looking, loud-mouthed jock, though Julie was nice enough, in a motherly way. A manicurist with extremely long nails, she carried an emery board as she made her way around the house, cleaning and bringing us hot cocoa and potato chips.

At one point, Rick sat at the edge of the couch, teasing us. He knew what we were up to and was set on giving us a hard time.

"You know, John's a virgin, too," he told me, and I felt myself blushing.

Later that night, Julie showed us to our room. It was upstairs, with a large, fluffy white bed. On one of the pillows lay a small black basket filled with condoms, compliments of either Rick or Julie, maybe both.

We undressed quietly, groped around clumsily, then got underneath the covers. It didn't take long; we were both too nervous for foreplay. In the middle of it all, I suddenly wanted to stop, but then I snapped and grabbed John's back, sucking him into me. One, two, three, four thrusts later, it was over.

Once he rolled off me, I got up and ran to the bathroom. I was breathing hard; the lights flickered into my eyeballs. I smelled weird. I smelled like John. I ran back into the room, where he sat up on the bed, naked, his legs curled under him.

"Are you okay?" he asked. He looked disoriented, blank. I nodded, looked at the white sheets, and ran my hands over them.

"There's no blood," I said, and for some strange reason, I began to cry.

I continued to visit John at his house. After he would wrestle Les out of the room, we would draw the shades, and then I'd pull down my pants while he pulled down his. Fully undressing was too risky, considering his twin had acquired the dirty habit of picking the lock.

Our bodies whacked back and forth as he thrust in and out of me. Though we had started telling each other "I love you," especially over the phone late at night, when we would express melodramatic agony for living in different school districts, the sentiment seemed very far away during the moments when we were having sex. We were suddenly lovers slipping out the back door of a smoky little bar, the woman hitching up her skirt as her man lustily yanks down her panties, then unbuttons his jeans and slides it into her discreetly. Back-alley sex, with gray, sullen skies and rain dripping over a ridged metal awning, the air turning heavy and thick.

We broke up ten months later, over the phone. He said he met someone else at school, some girl that played tennis. I informed him that I hated tennis and that I hated him as well, then slammed down the phone. Despite my professed anger, I felt nothing. I didn't understand it: I was supposed to be heartbroken. I was supposed to be shattered. Instead, I went to the fridge, made a sandwich, and watched TV.

Jack groaned, tensed, then grew limp. We stayed still for a moment, quietly breathing. Then I eased off him and grabbed a couple cigarettes, one for each of us. As we smoked, the moonlight crept silently over our skin.

In the postcoital silence, I felt nothing but loneliness. I was pretty sure that Jack felt the same way. Not that he would admit it. Instead, he said it was nice to be with someone who didn't pressure him. Someone he could drink with, play a few games of pool with. Someone he could fuck with no strings attached. And I was that person, with no hooks trying to snag him. He thought I was great because I didn't ask too many questions. Questions about Where We Stood In This Relationship, about whether he loved me. We didn't play that stupid relationship game, acting like we owed each other something. And I even agreed with him when he brought it up and said yes, it's a good setup, isn't it. The truth was that I felt nothing, and I hadn't felt anything in a long time, nothing for him, or for anyone else.

Dazed and tired, I got up and began looking for my clothes.

"Why don't you sleep here?" he offered with a yawn. "I mean, it's late and the buses don't run too often."

"Not tonight, it's fine. I'll walk."

I mumbled a good-bye once I was dressed, then scratched around, trying to find the front door. He got up to follow me, still naked. I found the front door and opened it just as he was asking if anything was wrong.

"I'm fine."

"Are you sure?" he asked, pulling a strand of hair away from my eyes.

"I'll see you soon," I said. I muttered another goodbye and walked away quickly, hearing the door click shut behind me.

Halfway down the block, I looked back at the gray Victorian, almost expecting him to be standing outside in the nude, watching me as I walked away. But no one was there. I wanted so much to cry, but nothing came.

four

When I finally managed to land my first dance in the VIP room, it was for a couple. After I'd finished dancing a set, they waved me over to their plush booth where they were sitting huddled together.

I rarely saw couples at Glitterati's, and when I did, it was always weird because I never knew the dynamic between them. Were they there for him or her? Was this something they'd discussed extensively before finally deciding to try it out? I'd always picture a married couple, straight-laced and slightly older, sitting in a therapist's office, discussing the problems of their (nonexistent) sex life. "There's a lack of arousal," they complain to the therapist. "We don't try anything new." The therapist brightly urges them to try something completely different: "How about one of those gentlemen's clubs? A really nice, classy one. You know. Upscale." They talk about it for a few more sessions, then decide to come to Glitterati's.

However, the couple beckoning me over didn't look straight-laced, though they were significantly older. The man, dapper and stylish, his gray hair slicked back with pomade, lovingly cradled a fat cigar between his manicured fingers. Under his black suit, the top three buttons on his shirt were undone, and a few gray chest hairs peeked out.

The woman looked even older but was trying really hard to look young. Straight blue-black hair fell to her large white breasts, which were frantically stuffed into a tight black velvet dress covered with tiny rhinestones. Her eyeliner was cat-pointy at the edges, and her mascara was globbed on. My hands looked like a young peasant's by comparison when she leaned over and took them into hers, her glossy, dark red nails gleaming, her fingers dripping with large, sparkling rings. A mix of hair dye and perfume filled the air when she flicked her hair off her shoulder and introduced herself as Candy, then introduced the man, her husband, as Carl.

"Just loved your act," Candy purred, then winked at me. A waitress in a white bistro apron approached the table and took our drink order. Candy ordered a brandy for Carl and a whiskey sour for herself. I ordered a Cabernet.

"Where are you from, dear?" Candy asked me as she took out a cigarette. Carl reflexively took a brass Zippo from his jacket pocket and lit it with a quick flick.

When I told her that I was born in Egypt, her eyes widened dramatically, the smoke rolling out her slick red lips.

"I told you so," she said as she playfully jabbed Carl in the ribs. He raised his eyebrows, grinned, and puffed out smoke rings.

She turned back to me. "Carl thought you were from South

America, but I told him, 'No way, José! She's probably from one of those places with belly dancers, where women can really shake their hips.' " She wiggled in her seat a little and then winked at me. Apparently, she and Carl had come into town from Las Vegas for business, but she didn't elaborate on what kind of business and I didn't ask.

"Las Vegas is fun, but it's getting too blonde," she said, flicking ash carelessly into a big, round crystal ashtray. "We love dark hair." She cast a sly look at Carl and he nodded, briefly touching her hair with a wistful look.

She leaned in and took hold of my hand again. "You've just got the most fabulous thick, black, wonderful hair."

I smiled politely.

When our drinks arrived, Candy insisted on a toast. "To a wild night," she rasped with a wink as we clinked glasses. She turned to Carl and winked to him as well. He looked at me and winked. I resisted the urge to wink and instead made small talk about music, movies, and San Francisco's outstanding public transportation. I was nervous because I knew they'd agree to my dancing for them if I asked. I'd almost gotten used to the idea that I might never get a VIP dance, and on some level almost accepted it. My small talk was a distraction from this discomfort, but I was a caught fish struggling in vain to slip off a very sharp hook, which was Candy and Carl, and the way they looked at me. Especially the way Candy looked at me. She reminded me of a retired burlesque dancer, and she may well have been, with her name and getup. She stared at me like I was a lollipop she wanted to lick up and down. This made me hide my face behind the wine glass—a bad habit I had when I was anxious.

Carl, on the other hand, was a spotless gentleman. He stood up when Candy excused herself to go to the bathroom, obediently flicked his Zippo whenever she took out a cigarette, and nodded, smiled, or raised his eyebrows when he heard something he approved of, like us having a wild night or ordering another round of drinks, or any time Candy commented about my hair. However, he never spoke for himself—Candy did all the talking.

"Carl and me would love to have you dance for us, darling."

I smiled and played with the stem of my glass, then touched my hair. "Of course," I finally said, then motioned to the back room.

"Ooh," Candy's glossy red lips puckered into a delighted little 'O.' "I wondered what that room was for. It's the naughty room!" She nudged Carl and he raised his eyebrows, gave a smile and a lengthy nod, and then put down his cigar. We downed our drinks, and I led them to the VIP room.

Inside the dimly lit red room, the dancers struck slow, sultry poses as they playfully whispered into the ears of their gentlemen admirers. I led Candy and Carl to a small corner couch and sat next to them, waiting for the song to end and a new one to begin. She smiled coyly as he snaked his arm around her waist and pulled her in close. While they nuzzled I thought that maybe dancing for a couple would be easier; at least they could distract each other and wouldn't be paying too much attention to me if I screwed up.

When a new song started, I peeled off my dress too quickly, folding it over and over again into a little square. Down to the bare basics of black bra and G-string, I stepped away from Candy and Carl and began to dance, trying to keep my timing slow and sensuous. I flipped my hair around my face and piled it on top of my head with both hands. This might've been interpreted as sexual if my hands, hips, and legs weren't all moving way too quickly.

They, however, seemed to think I was perfect. Carl's mouth opened and closed slowly while his hand crept up the black-fishnet-covered thighs of the agitated Candy. She spread her legs a little, moistened her red mouth, and began to writhe. I moved in closer to them, to Carl's side, careful not to touch him, my ass almost brushing his face. I could feel his breath on it, hot and frequent. I moved to her side and felt her hair on the outside of my thigh as she began to murmur about my hair, my hair, all that dark hair.

"Imagine it all over us, baby, falling over us," she said, caressing her own dyed hair, spreading her legs a little wider, hiking up her dress a little higher as Carl's hands moved from her waist to her breasts. She moaned loudly and he grunted in reply while a few of the men in the room shifted their heads in our direction. I just played with my hair and tried to keep from laughing. The more I played with my hair, the more Candy talked about it, the more Carl's hand squeezed her breasts and the louder she moaned. A couple dancers now turned toward us, distracted because their customers were distracted.

The song faded with Candy loudly moaning and drowning out the last few notes. I dressed quickly and hovered over them, not sure what to do next. When the next song began, Carl got up and placed forty dollars into my hand.

"Thank you so very much," he said clearly. I was stunned to hear his voice for the first time. He helped Candy up, smoothed the hair out of her face, and pushed her dress down over her fishnets. Placing his arm around her limp frame, he escorted her out of the room. I followed them out to the main floor and watched as they headed slowly back to the booth where I had found them. Carl threw a couple bills down on the table and collected their coats, and they walked past me on their way out of the club.

Princess walked over, adjusting the straps on her filmy red dress. "Looks like they were having fun," she said. She smelled like warm apple pie.

"Seemed like it," I replied, sticking the money into my bra. The gesture made me feel like I was working in a brothel.

As I was contemplating whether I should buy a purse, I felt a tap on my shoulder. It was the baboon-bouncer, guardian of the VIP room. Holding a clipboard in his hand, his spiked hair lethally shiny and sharp, he asked me for the club's cut from the dance. I gave him a ten.

"You owe another ten," he informed me, rubbing a nostril with his thumb.

"But I only did one dance," I argued. Then I remembered: The ten-dollar fee per dance was also per person. Irritated, I reached into my bra, pulled out another ten, and shoved it into his hand. He took the two tens and stuffed them in his suit pocket, then marked something on his clipboard.

"What's that for?" I asked, leaning in to look.

He pulled the clipboard away and told me that it was a list of all the dancers, with check marks next to their names for every time they did a dance. "That way we keep track of how much you guys owe the club, how good you do," he said. "But it's confidential info." He then walked away stiffly, back to the VIP room.

Why was it confidential? Pissed off, I turned toward the stage where some blonde was doing her thing. The club wasn't busy, and a handful of men sat watching her. The woman, tall and sturdily built, seemed to be dancing for one customer in particular, a gray-haired man wearing thin glasses and a dark suit, who sat alone at the far corner of the stage. He had already placed four twenty-dollar bills at her feet. When she removed her bra and her large breasts dropped heavily, he put down two more twenties, each one folded lengthwise. On the opposite side of the stage, the other customers added a few bills every time he did, as if they were in some kind of competition, even though they were only putting down one-dollar bills instead of twenties. The dancer didn't acknowledge them.

When the song ended, she collected her tips with a smile, put her clothes on, then, arm in arm with her big tipper, she headed to the VIP room. Princess was standing by me again, wearing a new outfit, a shiny blue dress with silver streaks.

"That's Arianna, she's usually a daygirl," she said. "That guy Phil's been her regular for about two years now. He always comes here for lunch and gets dances with her and her alone, but he pissed her off because when she was on vacation, he got a dance with Mia." Princess pointed at another tall, voluptuous blonde sitting with a customer at a nearby booth.

Trying not to sound too ignorant, I casually asked Princess

about regulars. How did dancers usually go about landing one? Did she have one?

"Not anymore," she said. "I used to, but it's difficult these days. Good regulars are hard to get, but you can't really force it. It's just the kind of thing that happens when you're not really trying." People always said that when they met the right person and fell in love; it just happened when they least expected it. It was strange to say the same thing about finding a regular at Glitterati's.

Princess went on to say that there were good regulars and okay regulars. The okay ones bought a few dances from the same girl but also sampled other women. A good regular, she said, stayed with you and was loyal. It sounded like a comparison of boyfriends: Some were good for long-term relationships; others screwed around and were not to be taken seriously.

"Phil's pretty much got a thing for blondes," she said, smiling. "I've tried to land him as a regular, and he was nice about it, but I found out I wasn't his type."

I stared at her silky, dark skin, sleek hair, and curvaceous body. How could she not be somebody's type?

"He's been coming in for a long time, about four years, since about the time I started working here. His last girl was Samantha, and they were together for two years, but then she moved to Ohio and got married. He was all depressed for a while, but then he met Arianna. He pays for everything, her car, her vacations." Princess walked off to the deejay booth to check her music before getting onstage to dance her set.

As I watched her move across the floor like a delicate figurine, too precious to be touched, I thought about getting a regular. It seemed to require a lot of strategy, as well as a kind of detachment. It was an ability that most of the dancers at Glitterati's seemed to possess, and I admired them for it, because I didn't posess it myself. Wasn't this how Buddhists attained enlightenment, by remaining detached and devoid of the stickiness of emotions? Detachment was precise, like a surgeon with a gleaming scalpel who knew exactly where to make the incision, while the patient lay there in complete surrender. I wished I could make them all surrender to me.

five

The dressing room at Glitterati's was always like a beehive of queen bees buzzing around in their prettiness. Still a drone, I put on a new purple dress that zipped up one side and featured a slit that shimmied all the way up my right thigh. I put on my makeup, mussed my hair, pleased that it was finally getting longer, and, for the final touch, took out a small black purse I had bought the day before.

The club was occupied by a small group of men who sat slumped over their dinner plates, cutting through steaks and shoveling forkfuls of sautéed something into their mouths. A woman I'd never seen before danced onstage. I watched her with interest, trying to memorize the movements of her body. Most dancers watched other dancers when they were onstage. I didn't know why–maybe sizing up the competition? For me, it was simple education; I wanted to learn to be a better dancer.

She looked like most of the other women at Glitterati's, same kind of clothes, same kind of hair. But she possessed an element

I hadn't witnessed in my four months of dancing. It wasn't that she was a good dancer; based on pure technical proficiency, she wasn't. The difference was that, under the stereotypical baby-doll makeup and little red costume, her body moved with a smoothness I'd never seen before. She willed the song into herself, bent each note with her knee or elbow. What she wore and how she looked were meaningless. She let go of her body and, with each note rising from the speakers, she was guided by an invisible thread stitched through her limbs, making her move with complete freedom and ease. This was surrender, total surrender of the body to the music. I had once surrendered to music like she did, but I hadn't yet found the courage to do it while naked onstage.

She kicked one leg into the air and bent her entire upper torso down to the side, when I noticed something dangling out of her G-string panties. It was a white tampon string. I dashed to the foot of the stage and waved her over; she didn't notice me, as she continued high-kicking and twirling and gyrating. I waved again, and she finally danced over. I pointed to her dangling string. She looked down, then back up, gave me a lopsided smile, mouthed a thank-you, tucked in the string, and then went on dancing like nothing had happened. I warily looked around the room and noticed a couple other dancers snickering.

When her song ended, she came over to me.

"I'm Edie," she said.

"I'm Rania," I replied.

Over the next two weeks, I saw Edie a few more times. I learned that she'd been dancing for four years and was enrolled in art school.

She told me that she was studying to be a sculptor, and I believed it when I saw her hands, which were unlike any woman's at Glitterati's; muscular, with light veins slightly protruding from her wrists up the length of her arms. I also learned something else about Edie when she began coming on to me in the dressing room.

"Do you like women? Are you bisexual?" she asked in a low voice, leaning into me. "Wait. Don't tell me." She cocked her head to her shoulder and inspected me through slit eyes that reminded me of a sleepy cat's. Then she nibbled on a grubby cuticle and smiled.

I had called myself a lesbian for about a year, after I first moved to San Francisco. I was tired of men, and my two dyke roommates at the time kept telling me strange, erotically charged lesbian stories.

I became curious and started sniffing around clubs, and I encountered women who looked more like adolescent boys than adult females. This was the look my roommates went for, the look I went for too. I stopped using makeup, cut my hair short, wore fake mustaches, stuffed rolled up socks in the crotch of my pants, and performed in lesbian clubs wearing men's suits, singing songs like "Luck Be a Lady." I attracted weird groupies: old, burned-out queens who asked me to escort them to disheveled clubs, and young, girlish, up-and-coming lesbians who batted their eyes at me. I became something of a "drag king," and when I wasn't wearing my glue-on mustache and rolled-up sock-crotch, I was hanging out at bars, usually the Volt, wearing pin-striped suspender pants and tailored white shirts (with the sleeves rolled up), with a black fedora tilted over one eye.

I had stopped dating men altogether (except for Jack, who, for some reason, didn't count), and began seeing women exclusively. But no matter how hard I tried, I couldn't get into it. Once I attempted a one-night stand with a butch girl. We pawed at each other in her dark bedroom, then undressed, got into bed, and started kissing (but not with tongue, because my dyke roommates advised against it). I tried to find the kissing pleasurable, but it wasn't. Maybe it was a lack of chemistry, too much drink, or too much darkness. But there was nothing erotic about it. The woman looked like my best friend from the fourth grade, a boy named Christopher, and her lips flapped like rubber bands against my mouth. After a while, I squirmed away, not knowing what else to do. She turned on the light, sat up in bed, and told me she really liked me and wanted us to get to know each other better. I nodded stupidly because, well, is there a graceful way to tell someone that you aren't sure if you're attracted to their gender?

After a few agonizing hours, I caught a cab (which she paid for) and promised to call (which I didn't). When I got home, I told my roommates about my date, and they had a good laugh, saying I'd experienced what was commonly known as a "Meet and Merge." Then they told me what they claimed was an old lesbian joke: "What does a lesbian bring on her second date? A U-Haul."

But now there was Edie. Edie the sculptor, putting herself through art school by stripping. Edie the indifferent, who never gave a damn about what people thought. A long-legged platinum blonde with a steely gaze. Edie, who scared the shit out of men even though she rarely said a word to them. As a stripper, she was a failure because she never made any money. Maybe men didn't think she needed any, because Edie didn't look like she needed anything from anybody. But here she was, in a place where need ruled. Here she was, Edie the mesmerizing, and I listened to Cab Calloway at home:

> Edie was a lady,
> Though her past was shady,
> Edie had class with a capital "K."

Dancing became a different experience for me because of her. I couldn't borrow her moves, because I wasn't Edie. But she lent me her confidence, and with it I became more courageous onstage. No longer feeling threatened, I rediscovered a self I'd tucked away under layers of doubt. I found my own body slowing and my eyes pausing and searching the faces of the men who watched me. And then, slowly, unlike for Edie, the money started coming in for me.

six

A few weeks later, Edie urged me to switch clubs with her, to a new place in the Financial District called Ruby's. News travels fast among strippers, especially news about clubs in better locations with promises of a steadier (and wealthier) clientele. The clientele at Glitterati's was wealthy but by no means steady—most of the businessmen looking for "upscale entertainment" didn't like venturing through the tangled jungle of North Beach sleaze to get to the club.

In addition, Glitterati's nightly dancer's fee was exorbitant: fifty dollars, plus ten percent of our earnings went to the deejay. And this did not include the doormen or security, who were looking to get tipped anywhere from ten to twenty dollars per dancer.

At Ruby's, the dancer's fee was only twenty-five dollars per night, plus a flat ten dollars for the deejay. There also was a tip for the "club mother." Stationed in the dressing room, the club mother was a fixture at most clubs. Usually an older woman, she was always equipped with extra lipstick, breath spray, gum, perfume, tampons, lotion, aspirin, and anything else a dancer may have forgotten to bring from home.

The club mother, whom I always had the urge to call den mother, was also there for any dancer having a personal crisis. She was supposed to act as an anchor, lending an ear to any problems or complaints a dancer might have. A dancer could tip her whatever she thought fair.

There were two bars in Ruby's: one downstairs in the main area, near the stage, and another upstairs, on the VIP floor. In contrast to the little room at Glitterati's, the VIP room at Ruby's took up an entire floor and was almost half the size of the area. The deejay booth was also upstairs, tucked away in a little corner. From the upper level, a dancer could look down over the rail and checkout anyone new who had just come in.

The manager of the club was a heavyset guy named Mike who had been sent out west from the New York location. He was kind and likable, with a sense of humor and a deep laugh. Even better, he genuinely wanted to help the dancers and actually listened to our suggestions. When I asked him if I needed to cover my tattoos, he shrugged and said that was my own decision. Finally, I had a chance to experiment with my image.

There was a broader sense of freedom at Ruby's: We had Mike, with his relaxed attitude, we could play whatever music we wanted, and we could do floor work, which had been forbidden at Glitterati's. Though we did have a set schedule, working a minimum of three nights per week, we weren't required to do lineups. Because of this freedom, I was able to make more money at Ruby's than I had at Glitterati's. My wardrobe grew to six impressive, pricey costumes, plus three good pairs of dancing shoes.

Somehow Edie managed to avoid having a set schedule like the rest of us. She would disappear for weeks on end, then reappear out of the blue. I'd go downstairs to the dressing room to freshen up after dancing a set onstage, and suddenly there she was. She'd walk up to me and, without a word, start applying a tube of pale purple-gray lipstick to my lips. "Junkie's lips," she would whisper while gliding it on. "That's what I call this lipstick color."

One Friday night, Edie asked me to accompany her to a party she'd been invited to. We left the club early, joined by a new dancer named Cindy, a blonde with a needy baby face and a pair of gigantic (false) boobs. Needless to say, she did extremely well as a stripper with this combination.

I was a little thrown when I saw her tagging along, because I thought it was only going to be Edie and me. I managed to make my face a blank mask as the three of us climbed into Edie's tiny white convertible, Cindy sitting in the back. After checking her face in the rearview mirror, Edie turned to me.

"Kiss me," she said. It was really more of a command, and I acted as though I didn't hear her. But I could feel Cindy's eyes burning into the side of my head from the back seat.

"Kiss me," she repeated, grabbing my hand. "On the lips."

I leaned over from the passenger seat and gave her a brief little kiss on the lips, like a bird darting down to pick up a bread crumb. She wasn't happy with this. In fact, she seemed downright offended. She started the car abruptly, and we were off into the cold depth of the November night.

We drove in silence, save for the whirring of the car's engine, so loud it made everything else vibrate. I would occasionally nonchalantly half-turn around to look at Cindy, who glared at me like she wanted to cut off my tongue with her teeth. Then I looked at Edie; her eyes were focused on the road and her competent hands gripped the steering wheel, white-knuckled, as she shifted gears angrily.

The cold air was charged with a piercing hostility. I knew this energy, knew its distinct bitter flavor. Feminine anger, so different from male anger, like a silver arrow heading toward its target. I huddled down in my seat, trying to shield myself from the wind and the imaginary arrows that were sinking into my skin.

Eventually, we pulled into the driveway of a large house, then entered a shabby living room that smelled like cats, with half-finished paintings of nude women and men and several art brushes still stiff with paint piled in the corners. Nearly all the furniture was eerily draped in white cloth. A thick, strange coat of orange stained the floor; I couldn't figure out if it was paint or cat pee.

There were six of us all together: the three of us, plus the owners of the house, Ralph and Nash, a gay couple Edie knew from art school, and Lara, a Wiccan clad in black lace and wearing a silver pentagram necklace.

After being introduced, Edie, Cindy, and I sat quietly on the couch. Cindy wouldn't even look at me, which was a relief.

Lara smoked a large, messy-looking joint, while a white Persian cat slept contentedly in Nash's lap. A large pile of cocaine sat in a black ceramic bowl on the purple coffee table, as if it were a complimentary plate of chips and salsa put out for the guests.

Edie helped herself to some and then asked me if I'd ever had a cocoa puff. I shook my head, then watched as she made me one, carefully twisting the cigarette paper to release the tobacco into a little pile on the table. She scooped up some coke with her car key and gently mixed it into the tobacco pile, then stuffed it all back into the cigarette paper, fitting in as much as possible. She handed it to me with a smile, and I took it, lit it, and took a drag.

Wow.

"Like it?"

I was impressed with the recipe. The combo was mellow but it had a fiery kick in the heart. I turned to Edie, wanting to tell her that she reminded me of a cocoa puff. She made one for herself, and pretty soon everyone was doling out a little bit of coke into their rolled-up dollars, or their fingernails, and sniffing politely.

A mindless conversation began about art school. At some point, Nash got up, gently placed the fluffy cat on Ralph's lap, and headed to the stereo. No part of the comatose animal moved during this transfer except for its collar, which jingled when Ralph ran his hand from the cat's head to its neck.

Suddenly, Edith Piaf's voice rippled from the stereo. As Lara tried to croak along in broken French, Edie casually threw an arm around my neck and pulled me close to her. Cindy, seeing this, began whining. "I want a cocoa puff too, Edie. Please make me one, please?"

Edie puffed out some smoke and cast Cindy a withering glance. "Make yourself one," she said, irritated. "I've already shown you how. Don't play dumb." Cindy's great sad eyes, not unlike a cocker spaniel's, dwelled on Edie for a moment, then moved down to the cocaine bowl. She clumsily attempted to make a cocoa puff for herself, but she accidentally ripped the cigarette paper in the process. She quickly gave up with a heavy sigh, leaned her baby cheeks into her hands, then gazed out the window, longingly.

Edie and I sat together, holding hands like an old married couple. She looked at the bare wall in front of her, took a drag of the cigarette, and held it in for a moment, a few tendrils of smoke curling out her nose and lips. Then she exhaled and closed her eyes, her long lashes casting small shadows on the top of her cheekbones. No matter how much I was tempted, I tried not to look at her too much; I was afraid that if I stared at her as much as I wanted to, I would end up like Cindy. But I knew what Edie wanted from me, and was frustrated to not be getting, which gave me a shred of pathetic control, which was really what all this was about anyway.

The sun was rising by the time we dropped Cindy off at her apartment in Nob Hill. She tried to stall, suggesting breakfast, suggesting Edie help her hang pictures in her bathroom. But Edie didn't respond, and eventually Cindy whimpered a thank you for the ride, her large eyes brimming with fat tears as we drove off. I wondered why Edie had bothered to invite her at all.

Soon we were parked outside my place as we smoked the last

of our cocoa puffs. My heart beat quickly—what if she wanted to come upstairs? She would see my crummy room with its crummy furniture. I didn't even have bookcases. I had milk crates. Stolen milk crates. She would see that I had no blinds, no curtains, no way to stop the daylight from glaring in, no way to stop Edie from seeing me without the face I'd worn throughout the night.

We sat in silence for a while, the engine still running, the heat turned up high to warm us against the chilly San Francisco dawn. Suddenly she turned toward me. I noticed that her makeup was faded, her face exhausted, like mine.

"I don't have sex," she said. "I'm not good with it, all the touching and stuff."

"I understand."

We said nothing for a while.

"How is it you can just accept that?" she asked suddenly. "Without knowing who I am, what my reasons are?"

I didn't know that I'd accepted anything. "Do you want to tell me your reasons?"

She shook her head. "It's not like that. It just seems kind of pointless trying to explain things that can't be explained."

"Right," I said, not understanding what she meant.

We sat in silence once again.

Finally, I got out of the car, dragging my bag of clothes limply behind me. I turned and watched as her car descended the slight hill, looking like the last scene of a movie, when the credits start rolling over the image and everything becomes letter-boxed before it all fades to black.

Egyptian Exotica

I stood alone in the street, costume bag in hand, listening to the sounds of morning: birds twittering, a dog barking somewhere, someone trying to start a car again and again and again. I lit a cigarette, dug in my pockets for my house keys, and listened as her name rose like lazy smoke in my mind: Edie, Edie, Edie. I unlocked the front door, went inside, shut the door behind me, and sat on the carpeted bottom step. Edie. Edie was her stage name. I'd never even asked what her real name was.

seven

On my way to the deejay booth one evening to pick out my music, I caught sight of myself in one of the club's many mirrors. The rhinestone-and-diamond choker on my neck shed tiny droplets of light onto my collarbone; the two high slits, one on either side, on my leopard-print mesh dress revealed my legs all the way up to my hips. I pulled matching gloves up to my elbows and, somewhat startled, thought to myself, Who is this woman, this creature, this figment of my imagination? A full-blown Athena springing out of Zeus's head, complete in armor. This sexpot!

I looked away from the mirror and chose my music, then got up onstage, where I swung around the pole while looking out at the club. A few guys sat around the stage, throwing down their bills and smiling as they sipped their drinks. The hot rhinestone choker forced tiny beads of sweat down my neck, which contrasted with the cool, smooth feel of the mirror against my back, ass, and legs. I was in a trance as I danced, and when the music stopped, the stage was covered with money. I picked up the bills and went downstairs.

When I returned upstairs, a chubby man waved me over to his table, then asked me to dance for him. I took him to the VIP room. Since it was busy, we had to share a couch with Misty, an ex-bodybuilder from Florida with a voice like Mae West, and her customer. Misty was a stripping veteran and had learned to perform with a kind of friendly detachment, methodically chewing gum as she rocked her body back and forth, then turned her backside to her customer and shook her hips.

The song playing was agonizingly long, something industrial. I danced for my customer, watching his pudgy face get sweaty with excitement when I leaned over and let my hair dangle in his face, his eyes bulging out like he was being strangled, his breath rancid, my body growing tense as his eyes burned into me. When I dangled my hair into his face again, this time closing my eyes to avoid his glassy gaze, I suddenly felt a clammy hand on my right breast. I snapped my body away, and he pulled his hand back as if he'd just been burned.

When the song ended, he gave me my money but no tip. Stunned, I thanked him politely and walked to the bar, where Misty was standing, guzzling a beer. I told her what had happened.

"That's how it works," she said. "Once in a while, you get an asshole. Sometimes you get a room of them, it's just the way it goes."

"But I don't get it."

"There's nothing to get, sweetie. Men can just be fucking pigs sometimes," she replied, sucking down more of her beer. Another dancer named Yvonne joined us and ordered a glass of wine while

Misty told her what had happened to me.

"What you need," Yvonne said, "is a regular. That's probably the best thing you can get, because if you get a good one, you can be more picky and not have to dance for guys like that asshole."

"Yeah, but there's always dirty bitches everywhere you go," Misty snorted. "That's just the way things are."

"What do you mean?" I asked.

"You know," Misty exclaimed, "dirty bitches who'll do anything! Hand jobs, fucking, whatever, you name it."

"Here?"

"Sure, here, there, and everywhere."

"Get a regular," Yvonne advised. "It's the best thing you can do."

"Do you have one?" I asked.

"Yvonne's got, like, four," Misty laughed. "She's set for life, but I don't have one. It's a real pain in the ass to find a regular these days. When I began dancing in Florida about ten years ago, I was getting fifties thrown on the stage, and some nights I walked out with almost a thousand dollars. I shit you not. I didn't need a regular back then because the guys were generous, and the clubs were always packed. Now I'm lucky to get a quarter of that." She polished off her beer. "It's changed, it's just not a good business like before because now they got too many clubs opening up. The only chance you get of making money nowadays is changing from club to club, because the guys like the fresh meat, and the new clubs are lenient at first, to get the girls in."

"Yeah, speaking of lenient, we have that mandatory meeting tomorrow," Yvonne chimed in.

"A mandatory meeting?" I asked. "What does that mean?"

"A mandatory meeting means that things are going to change. I hear Mike's out, and a new guy's coming in to run the club."

"What if I don't show up?" I asked.

"Then you're fired."

"They can't fire me," I protested hotly. "I pay to be here!" We all do, they reminded me.

eight

Twenty-odd strippers, many wearing dark sunglasses, stumbled in at ten-thirty the next morning, none in too good a mood about having to be up so early. We snarled our way to the coffee machine, grunting through complimentary bear claws, looking at each other strangely, trying to figure out who was who, since we rarely saw one another clothed.

It was surreal to be in a strip club in the morning, with all the lights on. Without the romantic softness of red and pink glowing from overhead, without the music, without the men, the place resembled a deserted cafeteria, with lighting reminiscent of the produce section at the grocery store. The barren stage stared blankly, the tables and chairs near it perfectly set, and everything was hushed and still as if nothing had happened the night before. For the first time, I noticed that the brass pole that ran from floor to ceiling in the center of the stage was actually not connected to the ceiling. I also noticed, amazingly for the first time as well, that there were no windows or clocks in the club.

A pile of booklets lay on one of the tables, below a sign that said, TAKE ONE PLEASE AND SIT DOWN! I grabbed one and sat at a table with Misty and Yvonne.

A man got up onstage and started pacing. His blond hair was greasy, styled in tight ringlets. He had beady eyes and a huge vulturelike beak for a nose, below which sat a cheesy, thick moustache. He wore silky, colorful clothes, and his pants made a low whooshing sound as he moved. When most of us were seated, he stopped pacing and eyed the room.

"I'm Tony," he began. "My job is to help you. To help you make you more money. Money's not always easy to make here, am I right?" A few dancers murmured in agreement. Tony beamed, obviously thinking that he was on the right track.

"I'm here to help you when you're having a problem with a customer. I'm here to keep you going when the going gets tough, and like you know, it can get pretty tough here sometimes. Isn't that right?" Again, a few murmurs of agreement.

"I know a-a-a-all about it. I've been in this business for a long, long, long time. I've seen it all in this industry, ladies. And trust me, I know what works and what won't. That's why I put together this little booklet here." He flashed the booklet at us.

"I want you to know as we go over these points that they aren't here just to make your life miserable. I mean, really." He slapped his knee. "Let's be honest. If you're unhappy, then there's no money, then I'm unhappy! These points are here because they will make your life easier. They're a foolproof method, a shortcut to making real money. Think of them as your secret weapons." He winked, then opened the booklet and began to read, but he was quickly interrupted when some of the dancers asked what had happened to Mike.

"Mike's gone," Tony said curtly.

"But why's Mike gone?" someone asked.

"Because Mike wasn't fulfilling his managerial duties."

"How was Mike not fulfilling his managerial duties?"

Tony flashed the booklet at us again.

"Because of this, ladies," he said, waving it around with biblical conviction. "Mike wasn't giving you the basics of what you needed to know, he wasn't doing his job properly, so now I'm here to set the record straight, to get things rolling in the direction they were meant to roll."

Misty, Yvonne, and I looked at each other warily.

"Listen to me, ladies," he said seriously, hands on his hips. "Upscale clubs can be very lucrative. I'm sure some of you already know this, but I'm here to let you in on some secrets that are going to make you a killing. I know everybody in this room wants to make more money." He gave the room a toothy smile. "So let's just go over these rules and regulations. Then I'll get into some methods to approach men that you've never even thought of. You know, every woman in this room is beautiful, but some of you make more money than others do. Do you think that's because one is more beautiful than the other? Of course not! It's just that some of you are smart about making money, and some are not."

Misty snapped her gum furiously.

"So let's start!" He took a quick sip of coffee from a little white Styrofoam cup and cleared his throat. "No gum chewing."

Misty snapped her gum loudly again, and Tony looked up as a few dancers tittered. He gave her a look, then went back to reading his booklet.

"No smoking while walking around. No visible piercings. All tattoos must be covered. No exceptions. Fees must be paid on time."

I raised my hand, feeling like I was back in a classroom.

"What is it?" Tony asked wearily.

"I have some really small tattoos on my shoulder," I said. "You can hardly tell they're there." A couple other dancers joined in and said that they also had some small tattoos and it was such a hassle to cover them up with makeup because it smeared onto the costumes.

Tony's ringlets shivered as he shook his head. "Trust me on this one. I'm telling you, no matter how great your tattoo is, or how cute you think it is, men always prefer the wholesome look. That's what sells here. This is an upscale place!"

Upscale. I was so tired of that word.

"Nothing, and I mean nothing, is sexier than unmarked skin. Trust me on that one. I'm a guy, and I know what guys respond to. I can guarantee you that those tattoos will only distract men and take away your money, because it disrupts the whole purpose of being here."

"And what purpose is that?" I asked.

"Fantasy," he said without missing a beat. "Mystique. Call it whatever you want, ladies, but that's it in a nutshell." I had a sudden overwhelming urge to gracefully walk up to Tony and strangle him.

Rania Zada

As he went on reading the manual, clicking off each rule guaranteed to make us oodles of money, every reason I'd left Glitterati's for Ruby's began to crumble: Twenty-five-dollar fine for being late to work. Twenty-five-dollar fine for leaving work early. Ten-dollar fine for being late onstage. Termination for repeatedly being late, or for repeatedly leaving early. An increase in the house fee to forty-five dollars per night, to be paid by nine o'clock each night, no exceptions. Then, the little gestapo details: No chipped nails or weird lipstick colors. No dying hair without management's approval (even Glitterati's never had that one). No catfights. No sloppy drunken behavior and no downing shots with customers. "If a gentleman insists on buying you a shot," Tony said, "you must sip it."

No fondling ourselves while onstage. No grabbing our nipples, our buttocks, our genitals. We could caress our outer thighs but not our inner thighs. We had to be at least six inches away from the tip rail when topless. Worst of all, the lineups were back. And, for added cruelty, the new lineups took Glitterati's three-minute song to an entirely new level, adding a form of torture called the Goodbye Song, during which, at the end of the night, we were supposed to get up onstage and throw kisses to the audience while making moony eyes. All these things were just the beginning, because Tony said he had some other tricks up his sleeve that promised both to promote the club and increase our income. I didn't want to know what else was in his little bag of tricks.

Many of the rules Mike had made us read and sign were standard in California topless clubs. But he didn't dwell on them; he only told us to read them and sign if we wanted to work at Ruby's. But with Tony, I got the feeling that he would soon be telling us there would be no horseplay in the halls, no roughhousing, no graffiti in the dressing rooms, and that all strippers had to have hallway passes and a signed note from Mom and Dad for field trips to the shoe store.

A few dancers tried to argue with Tony. It didn't seem fair, they pointed out; why did we have to have all these rules if we were paying to be here? If we were really independent contractors, as we stated on our tax returns, didn't we get to make our own rules? One dancer remarked that these rules existed in most upscale clubs she'd worked at, and that she'd followed them religiously, but they hadn't made a difference in her income. A few others agreed with her, then a chorus of female voices began to rise in protest, questioning Tony's booklet.

"You think I'm doing this for my own good, ladies?" he said with a stiff little laugh. "I have better things to do than sit there for hours and hours, typing up this stuff for you. I'm doing this because it works, and I know it works."

I imagined Tony up late at night, his greasy ringlets tied up in a purple scrunchie as he wildly tapped away on the keyboard, sweating over words, trying to phrase them in a nonoffensive manner, trying so very hard to please his ladies.

No.

I imagined Tony lounging on a tacky orange corduroy love seat, sipping a cappuccino, licking the froth off his greasy mustache as he read a fax of the rules sent to him from the central office in Dallas.

Yes.

"Now listen up," he said, rolling up his sleeves. "I've launched a lot of clubs, a lot of new clubs that needed that extra zing to really get the guys coming in. I've managed some pretty high-class clubs, like in Dallas, and let me tell you ..." He clapped his hands excitedly, like we were the audience for an infomercial. "We. Have. A blast. The girls are making at least six hundred a night and that's just weekdays. On the weekends, we're talking eight hundred, nine, a thousand. That's tax-free, ladies. I tell you, it's a party every night, and the crazy thing—everybody gets paid to party! We have a hell of a time trying to close the place down every night because it's packed!"

"But in Dallas you can dance nude," Misty reminded him. "I know, we had the same thing in Florida, and I know what you're talking about, because we could do topless dances and ..."

"Doesn't matter," he interrupted. "You can make that kind of money right here." He pointed to the ground with both hands, but it looked like he was pointing at his crotch. Then he stopped pointing and stared out at us with an earnest look on his face.

"I see how some of you are looking at me, and I'm not saying it's going to work for everyone. It's not going to work for a girl who doesn't care. It's not going to work for a girl who doesn't want to make money, real money. Hey, girls like that can go work in another club for all I care. One of those sleazy clubs off Market Street, where girls do God-only-knows-what to make money. Go on, go work over there, go sell your body on the streets for all I care. I only want the cream de lay cream. That's what I want. And that's what you should want for yourself, too, ladies."

That's crème de la crème, you idiot, I thought.

Two strippers, offended by either Tony's butchering of French or his car-salesman tactics, got up and left the meeting. Tony bid them farewell with a chilly smirk.

"Bye-bye. If any of you want to join them, go ahead."

I didn't move. And at the end of the meeting, I signed my name at the bottom of a piece of paper that said yes, I'd been told what the rules were, and yes, I knew what I must and mustn't do. I signed because I didn't know what else to do. I signed because I didn't have a game plan. I signed because even though part of me knew that Tony was full of shit, another part hoped otherwise. Plus, I didn't want to slink away and let him have the final say.

Fuming, I caught the bus home. The day was dreary and cloudy, with occasional raindrops. I was tired from only four hours of sleep, but my brain twitched in rebellion to Tony's demented pep talk. Who was he to tell me what to do? He said he knew what a man liked, and that his ideas of sexiness came from his male perspective, but from what I'd learned, what a man wanted was limited to whatever was presented to him. If Tony limited variety, then he limited fantasy. Maybe I was the one who knew nothing about fantasy, even though I was just that at Ruby's, four to five nights a week.

nine

Within two weeks, everything changed drastically. First, Tony hired an all-new security staff, made up of men who walked stiffly through the club wearing black suits, their hands crossed over their crotches like they were at a Mafia funeral. The head of security (which we didn't have before) was a strange little Vietnamese guy named Charlie, who, though nice enough, was maniacally chatty, a likely side effect of being on cocaine.

In addition to the new rules and the new security, Tony also replaced the club mother, the nice woman in her fifties, with a very young woman from Mexico named Maria, who spoke only a handful of words in English ("hello," "goodbye," and "tip"). Her chief accomplishments were twice spraying Mace in the dressing room, thinking it was perfumed body spray.

To top it all off, what most of us feared came true—more dancers were hired. Under Mike, Ruby's had employed about twenty dancers, which was a good number because it kept competition to a minimum, and women were a lot nicer to each other because there was plenty of business to go around. But now that Tony had hired another twenty dancers, things began to get pretty cutthroat as we all fought over the shrinking pool of money.

Most nights I began my shift by sitting at the bar with Misty and Yvonne, drinking wine to induce a buzz (a new rule of mine) as we bad-mouthed Tony and watched the new women he hired, mostly brought in from clubs he used to manage in Dallas and Arizona. They were all friendly in the dressing room and smiled at us in the hallway, but they congregated and mingled within their own sphere, walking around together and working customers together and giving each other looks only they could understand. They were a new species at Ruby's, and I couldn't tell one from the other because they all seemed to be the same creature.

Even after Misty and Yvonne would leave the bar, I would still sit there by myself, watching the new dancers as I drank. And drank. I had always drunk a little in the past, sometimes between sets, but it suddenly seemed so much more important, more urgent.

Though I acted like I knew what I was doing, I still trembled on the inside when I had to approach men for dances. I felt like they could see my trepidation, my fear. I thought of Edie and how she never looked like she needed anything, radiating a silent statement that said, I don't need, I want, and you need to worry if I want you. She didn't make a lot of money, and I think it was for that reason. Men didn't come into the clubs for that. They wanted to forget that they needed approval, and, as a result, women's roles in the clubs were the opposite of what they were in the outside world: They had to pretend they needed. In bars, at home, out there, I needed nothing. But in the club, I had to pretend to need in order to survive. And I had to pretend to want as well, because I both wanted and needed the money.

As a result, I began to descend into dark moods when I worked, full of hatred for myself, the club, everything that was alive but appeared dead, only to look alive when it was wound up with a fake gold key. I drank and drank, but I couldn't get drunk because the adrenaline of anger was pumping through me too fast.

One night I watched as Vixen, one of Tony's recruits, a silicone-implanted blonde with fattened lips, stripped down to a black G-string and top hat while wiggling and squirming to "You Can Leave Your Hat On," by Joe Cocker. The men cheered her on and threw down bills while blasting whistles through their fingers. I realized that Tony was trying to transform the club into something cute and playful, which was the opposite of my look and style.

My anger increased. I approached four men. I got rejected four times. I was no Vixen to them. I hated how my confidence level was so attached to how much money I made. I hated that how much money I made was so attached to my confidence level.

Then my body began to feel off when I was up onstage, like someone had turned off a switch in me. I'd heard that it was normal to have off nights as a dancer, nights when you weren't attuned to the crowd. But I didn't like it, not when my financial well-being depended on being "on" all the time.

I began to crumble, then became ashamed that I was crumbling.

Then I got pissed off that I was ashamed. Then I just snapped. The next guy that turned me down received the full brunt of my wrath.

"Who the fuck do you think you are?" I exploded. He didn't react to my anger, instead adjusting his glasses while he continued looking at the stage. I planted myself next to him and stared at his profile. Then I stared down at his hands. He had long fingers, typing hands. I saw the wedding band.

"So," I started, lighting a cigarette, "does the old ball and chain know you're here?"

He didn't answer.

"What's the point of you leaving your ring on anyway?" I asked with irritation. "Please leave me alone," he pleaded. "I don't want a dance."

"I'm not asking for a dance."

"Then what do you want?" He still wouldn't look at me.

"I want to know why you think being here is going to solve your problems."

"I don't have a problem!" he said, his voice growing louder.

"Right," I said, blowing smoke in his face.

"It isn't any of your damn business," he spat out, still watching the stage.

"Ooh," I laughed. "God forbid you actually make some human contact with one of us, or talk like a regular fucking human being. It's all about these fucking games so you can forget the life you chose for yourself but don't want anymore."

He told me to go fuck myself. I told him that I'd rather fuck myself than fuck him. Then I stormed off and headed to the dressing room. What was wrong with me?

The dressing room was deserted. I changed out of my work outfit and into my regular clothes. Fuck you, Tony, I thought as I slipped on my jeans and sweater. It felt so good to wear clothes at that moment, so good to not be naked.

I crammed my things into a bag and tore out of the dressing room, out of the club, ignoring the mafioso security guys yelling after me as I shoved the door open with my steel-toe boot. Fuck you. I knew I'd be fined for going home early. I just didn't give a shit.

ten

Living in Los Angeles as a girl of fifteen, so close to the glitz and glam of Hollywood, I'd dreamed about being carried away by the man of my dreams. Tall and handsome, he would sweep me away on a white horse so we could be together always and forever. The fairy tale.

Living in Los Angeles at nineteen, I got Brian, a guy with a gritty face and bony frame who swept me off my feet and onto the back of his loud, rattling motorcycle. Our affair lasted two whole days, two days of being high on coke and speed and never sleeping.

We met at a party, and when he gave me my first snort of speed, it was love, love, love. Brian became The One, and without another word, I was flying through the Santa Monica Mountains. The burn of speed and the yellow gravel in my nose made me want to cry in agony, but something overrode the pain; it was like I was inhaling the world through my nose, taking in every molecule and vibration in the air. Everything had sharper lines, the stars screamed, the wind rubbed through my jeans, my shirt, into my bra. Or was that Brian's hand?

Before I said goodbye to him (I never saw him again), we took a shower together. In the hot spray of water, two days of grime, road dust, sweat, and lack of food were drowned out by our deafening heartbeats. We stood together, naked, laughing, crying, singing, wailing. It wasn't a shower; it was a vast, endless ocean with the sun reflecting off its surface, and we were swimming in all of it.

Then he was gone. But something of him remained—the drugs. The way they danced around in my blood made something happen inside me, like a resurrection of faith and possibility. Everything ebbed and pulsed. I could finally feel. I was nineteen, fit, and hungry, and I begin to take just about every drug I could get my hands on, except for heroin—which didn't seem like a recreational drug but like something that required an emotional commitment.

At the time, I was working as a cocktail waitress at a strip club called the Seventh Veil, off Sunset Boulevard in Hollywood. I made a ton of money there and spent a ton of money everywhere, mostly on expensive clothes.

After work I would go to a late-night diner off Hollywood Boulevard to eat and write in my journal. At this diner, I also struck up friendships with many of the homeless kids that frequented the area, mostly runaways from other parts of the country. I quickly began absorbing their lives, visiting the dilapidated buildings where they squatted, sometimes taking them into my own apartment to live for a while.

In exchange for my feeding and housing them, they became my main drug connections, introducing me to the right dealers, helping me get the good stuff. And because I often couldn't commit to a bag of anything, I always ended up sharing, which made everyone very happy and me very popular.

However, I didn't bother paying rent for my apartment on a regular basis, which made me unpopular with my landlord and got me evicted. It wasn't that I couldn't afford to pay; I just didn't want to be bothered with paying rent when I had many pretty things to buy.

I wound up quitting my waitress job at the strip club, as well as my homeless friends and most of the drugs that went along with them, and moving back home. My mother nagged me to get a real nine-to-five job, but I'd become accustomed to having cash in hand, so an office job was out of the question. Besides, I'd had a couple of them right after high school, and I detested sitting behind a desk. One day, while looking through the classifieds section, I found an ad for taxi dancing. It seemed harmless, no nudity, so I began working in a sleazy downtown club, much to my mother's chagrin.

We would sit in a line of chairs and wait as the men, seated on the opposite side of the room, surveyed us before approaching. It was like a demented school dance, with hours of stupid, misdirected eye contact until we were swept away to dark corners to wrestle with men trying to grind their dicks against our thighs. It was degrading and really nasty, but at the time I didn't see it as anything more than annoying.

My taxi-dancing career only lasted for a few weeks, however, mainly because of an English drug dealer named Robert. He was a regular at the club, and his mission was to sell the girls a few drops of GHB at five bucks a pop. He acted like a car salesman, bantering and bartering, carrying around a clear plastic bottle filled with the stuff in the pocket of his big black leather trench coat. GHB wasn't yet illegal. Weight lifters used it to beef up. But it gave me a nice floating buzz that made me feel like I was romping through a field of daisies. I would buy a few drops from Robert and slip them into my soda. It made me feel a bit sensual but nothing more.

One night, while buying a few drops, I snatched the bottle from his hands. He told me to give it back. I wouldn't, examining the liquid instead. Robert warned me that it wasn't a good idea if I was planning to drink the entire thing. I ignored him and unscrewed the plastic white top from the bottle. "Don't be stupid, put the bottle down," he said. I smiled at him, then guzzled the entire bottle. Robert gulped.

"You're fucked," he said. He grabbed the empty bottle from my hands and darted out of the club.

A short while later, I was blissfully dancing with a large hairy man, feeling a good buzz but nothing else. Robert had just been trying to scare me, I thought. I'd done heavy drugs, so what was the big deal about this one? I sipped happily on a soda and danced, feeling tipsy, fuzzy, and indestructible.

Then I blacked out.

I don't know how many hours later I woke up in the manager's office, screaming and hysterical, while somebody slapped my face hard. A wet washcloth was on my forehead. The fluorescent light of the office shrieked. I looked down at myself: There was vomit all over my dress. My ears ached. I remembered nothing. A woman I recognized as a coworker was wiping my face with the wet washcloth, then slapping me across the face. She stopped slapping when my eyes stayed open for good.

She explained that she was a certified nurse and that I'd dropped cold in the middle of the dance floor. The customer I was dancing with had thought I was dead, and she'd had to give me CPR because my heart had stopped beating. No one had bothered to call an ambulance because the owner was paranoid that the club would be shut down if they found a dead junkie in it. She looked disgusted with me, saying that if I didn't want to die, I should stop shooting up. But I wasn't a junkie, I explained. She didn't believe me.

Then the club owner stomped into the office. Jesus, did I know the kind of scene I'd caused? They'd had to drag my body off the dance floor. One girl had already quit because she was terrified. He didn't want no junkie bitch tainting his classy establishment. He told me to get the hell out and never come back.

I left quietly and steered clear of drugs for a while. I didn't want to die, but more important, I didn't want to be humiliated like that again. It was easy to stay clean; I was too fickle to commit to anything, even a drug habit. For the next three years, I had no desire to touch anything.

But now, suddenly, the nights always needed a few glasses of wine and sometimes a little more. One evening, Pam, a trashy miniature Barbie doll who lived in a dumpy little apartment with her kids and boyfriend and sold drugs on the sly at the club, and I slipped into the handicapped stall in the ladies' room and smoked crack together.

Wearing my latest glamorous attire, a silky, pink floor-length number with delicate spaghetti straps, I sucked, while Pam, smoothing a stray blond hair into place, held a lighter underneath the tinfoil. I inhaled through a hollowed pen and breathed in deeply, contemplating the true meaning of duality as the foul smoke hit my lungs. Then I breathed out, preparing myself for more magic upstairs.

eleven

"Layla," Tony called out from the hallway. He stood with his hands on his hips like a school principal. "Will you step into my office, please?" I entered his icy office, which contained a desk, a black leather swivel chair, and a bulletin board covered with Polaroids of women in bikinis.

"I called you in here because I've been meaning to have a word with you," he said, fingering a ringlet on his head. "You didn't cover your tattoos up tonight. I believe we discussed this at the orientation."

"I forgot," I replied.

"Ah, but it's not the first time you've forgotten," he said, folding his arms. "You've left them uncovered a few times already. At first I thought maybe you did just forget, but now, I don't think so."

"Actually, I did forget tonight," I said. "But I like my tattoos and—"

"Let me just get to the point, Layla," he interrupted as he swiveled in his chair. "You've disrespected me. By reading the rules and signing them, you've agreed to follow them, and when you decide to ignore them deliberately, you're disrespecting me, do you understand?"

I stared into his beady black eyes.

"As far as the rules go," he continued, "they're fixed. No changes, no exceptions. And they're for your protection, do you understand? This is an upscale establishment."

An upscale establishment where I smoked crack.

He pointed to the pictures of bikini-clad women on the bulletin board. "You see that? Do you know what those are?"

"Those appear to be women," I replied sarcastically.

"They're dancers, beautiful girls. And they're all on a waiting list, just dying to work here. Do you know why? Because this club is Something Big. Do you understand what Something Big is, Layla? Too many beautiful dancers want to work here for me to bend the rules just for you, do you understand?"

"Unfortunately."

"And you can drop the attitude!"

"Part of my charm," I mumbled.

Two weeks before Christmas, I booked a flight to Florida to see my family. Before I left, I worked several shifts in a row, trying to save up money to buy them presents. At night I dreamed of the Ruby's stage, specifically the brass pole that stood in its center. In my dreams, I grabbed hold of the pole with both hands, uprooted it from the floor, then planted it into different parts of the stage, until, finally, I placed it back in the very center of the stage, where it belonged. I had no idea what the dream meant.

A few days before I left for Florida, I ran into Jack at the Volt. We followed the usual scenario.

"Where are you these days?" he asked as we lay in bed having a postcoital smoke.

"What do you mean?"

He didn't say anything and turned to kiss me. I turned away. He looked at me for a long time.

"How's the dancing?" he asked. "They treating you all right?"

"It's okay."

He nodded and slipped under the covers. I got out of bed.

"You aren't sleeping here?"

"No." I looked around the dark room, grabbing at clothes until I found my own. "Not tonight."

"Okay."

I got dressed slowly. I thought maybe he'd tell me that he really wanted me to stay. But no, Jack never said that, never said, I really want. He never expressed authentic desire. That was the beauty of it all when we first became involved: no romance, no emotions. "Feelings complicate things," we used to say. We were both so evolved, so enlightened. Looking down on the world like a couple of bullshit gurus.

But now I was getting tired of this, tired of the fact that it was supposed to be such a great setup. It wasn't. It was preordained and contrived. And I was getting sick of being the duty-free fuck. If the concept of having what we had was because of the freedom it gave us, then it should encompass everything and not exclude specific things, like the possibility of commitment. But I couldn't say this because it would've freaked Jack out, and frankly, it would've freaked me out, too. I didn't even know if I wanted more than we had, but I was sick of what we did have.

I walked slowly to the front door.

"Bye," he called out. "Have a good Christmas."

"Yeah, you too," I said, closing the door behind me.

The flight to West Palm Beach was a red-eye, but instead of sleeping, I was restless, fidgeting in my seat as I flipped through the Sky Mall catalogue, reading about ridiculous gadgets and high-tech devices, all guaranteed to make my life easier: a heated ice-cream scoop, magnetic facial masks to pull snot out of my sinuses, electric nose clippers, electric cat feeders, and so on. Once I got bored with that, I looked out the window at the dark night sky, hypnotized by the steady, soft snore of the woman seated next to me. Finally, I fell asleep.

I'd never cared much for the holidays. They'd always been a lonely time, even for me, a solitary creature. I didn't have a steady circle of friends, and the holidays always emphasized how important it was to be surrounded by people, whether you liked them or not.

My family never really celebrated Christmas until I was ten, when my mother married my stepfather and we moved to England from Egypt. That Christmas was the first time I saw snow, and everything was covered in a thick, white, feathery blanket. We had a real Christmas tree, fat and generously strung with lights of all colors, and beneath it were packages wrapped in crisp silver, red, and gold paper. The fire was crackling, and I lay on the couch, sick with an earache, bundled up in blankets, watching Mary Poppins on TV.

I awoke as the plane began its descent. At first the sky lightened slightly, just a glimmer of sun behind the clouds. Within a few minutes, though, the sun blazed, and everything was a voluptuous orange.

I looked down at Florida, a strange and happy-looking place of tidy beaches, newfangled resorts, swimming pools, and palm trees. Everything looked oversize and systematic. Much like Los Angeles, without the mountains or smog.

I found my mother and stepfather at the baggage claim. She yanked me close and gave me a hug, enveloping me into her bright pink shirt, as my stepfather positioned his arms around my shoulders and gave me a polite pat on the back. Maybe it was the humidity, the Floridian heat with its sauna-effect summers, but both of them looked thinner and a bit wilted, as if all the air had been let out of them. My mother's eyes, hastily lined with black kohl, peered up at me, and I thought of how she used to look so much larger than life to me, and how she now looked like she'd somehow shrunk.

We collected my luggage, and my stepfather ran ahead to get the car. Left alone with my mother, I immediately lit a cigarette, feeling my head grow lighter with each puff.

"Are your boobs bigger?" she suddenly blurted out.

"Mom . . ."

"Well, they look bigger and so do you; you look a little stronger or something. What happened?"

"I got a boob job," I offered.

"You what?"

"I'm just kidding."

"You got a boob job? Why? When did this happen, why did you get one?"

"I said I was kidding."

She kept staring at my chest as my stepfather pulled up in the car.

We pulled into a dirt driveway, in front of a large ranch-style house. As we walked into the living room, a tabby looked up groggily from the couch. My mother shooed it off, and the cat jumped down, giving my mother one of those dirty looks cats are notorious for giving.

I sat down and was quickly greeted by the shy smile of Tiana, my two-year-old half-sister. I picked her up, then immediately put her down because she wasn't as light as she looked. She scampered around in little circles, while my other half-sister, Sara, and then my half-brother, Kyle, both in their pajamas, came out of my parents' bedroom. Sara was the oldest child from my mother and stepfather's marriage, twelve years my junior, followed by Kyle, fourteen years younger, and then Tiana, a full twenty years younger than me.

"Hi Rania," Kyle muttered in a high-pitched voice. With his olive skin, dark eyes, and dark hair, he looked the most like me of all the children.

"Hi Kyle," I copied in the same high-pitched voice, then mussed his hair with my hand. He made a face and jerked his shoulders and head.

"Hi," he said again, sucking in his cheeks and fiddling with his ear.

"Hi," Sara said, mimicking his high voice. He gave her a nasty look and she smirked at him.

Just then my grandmother pushed her way in past everyone. "My granddaughter, I want to see my granddaughter," she said in Arabic as her hands wrapped around mine. She pulled me to her, and I felt her small, thin body take me into another time. Her face may have been lined with age, but in her eyes, I could still see the woman I remembered from the photos she used to show me when I was a child. Pictures of her doing all kinds of things, from running meaningless errands to hosting glamorous parties, her hair a mass of black curls against a white complexion, her eyes gleaming like a woman sentenced to life in an asylum.

My mother used to say that my grandmother was born in the wrong time, in the wrong place. Egypt, 1916. A bad time for an ambitiously curious woman with looks and brains. She was an actress and had a ravenous compulsion for the stage and for knowledge, and that was not a good thing back then. If it were Massachusetts in the 1600s, she probably would have been burned at the stake. Instead, she was married off to a stranger twenty years her senior. Luckily, my grandfather was kind and patient and loved her for who she was. Even when she swore off Islam and claimed herself a Baha'i, he still loved her. Even when she took her children to Baha'i meetings and got arrested at protests, he loved her. Even when she spent her days going to matinees, watching

Hitchcock's *Rear Window* obsessively, leaving her two children at home to be attended by nannies, he loved her. And she was not an easy woman to love. She threw tantrums. She was trapped and uneasy and neglectful. Just like my mother. Just like me?

"How are you?" she asked in Arabic, touching my face and patting me on the cheek.

I nodded and smiled, but said nothing in reply. I had mostly lost the Arabic language after moving to the U.S. because my mother spoke only English to me. Though I had forgotten how to form coherent sentences, I could still understand what was being said.

My grandmother wasn't at all happy about this, and for good reason—she couldn't communicate with me anymore. Her eyes dropped and she looked at me with quiet disappointment.

"So," she said in Arabic, "you still can't speak."

"Oh, Mamma, leave her alone and stop making such a big deal," my mother, overhearing, exclaimed in Arabic.

"You say that? Language and communication hold families together," my grandmother remarked, also in Arabic, her finger poised at us. "Don't ever forget that."

I bit my lip, feeling ashamed, while my mother shook her head and sighed. My stepfather and the children looked at the three of us blankly, not understanding a word that was being said.

As the days passed, dancing slipped out of my mind. I watched a lot of television and sometimes played with the kids, not knowing what else to do with myself in Jupiter, Florida. I wrote in my journal and paced the house late at night like a restless ghost, prowling the hallways, watching my brother's and sisters' sleeping faces and my grandmother's frail body huddled under the covers in her bed. I wished I felt closer to them.

My mother and I began to bicker relentlessly. It was the way we'd always communicated, the same way she communicated with her own mother. I continually lost patience with her because she didn't really listen to what other people said, instead barking orders without caring about how her words came across, as if the part of her brain that filtered thought from speaking was broken. This was the way it had been for me growing up, a constant hailstorm of words and commands.

"Rania. Set the table. Put down some napkins." Pause. "Now."

"Rania, Rania. Don't sulk. Stop scribbling in that notebook. Now."

"Rania. I don't care if the ski mask makes you look like a bank robber. It's cold, wear it to school."

My stepfather was immune to this. He was a quiet man from Holland, and I found his stoic silence unnerving. He had a poker face, and he even cracked jokes without smiling. He would tease my mother affectionately, but she never knew whether he was kidding, and he never let on. He was a different breed from us. When I first met him, he radiated a calm that was at once endearing and mysterious. He spoke in soft tones with the touch of a European accent, and I had to lean in to listen every time he spoke.

By contrast, our Mediterranean background meant we let out a wallop every time we opened our mouths. In addition, since my mother and grandmother were constantly at each other's throats, the walls shook whenever they "spoke," especially in the kitchen while cooking. When asked why they were yelling, my mother would explain impatiently that they were "just talking."

Though this was perfectly natural behavior in Egypt, it appeared ill-mannered, even savage, when we moved to England, and it may have bothered my stepfather, or at least my mother thought it did. I could see her grow self-conscious every time her voice rose when he was in the room. If he was around and my grandmother or I were being difficult, my mother would say through clenched teeth, in a barely controlled voice, "Quiet. The man's home from work and needs some peace."

I would stare at her when she said this. Who the hell was this woman? I didn't know whether to be relieved that she wasn't screaming anymore or disappointed that she was hiding a part of herself. Sometimes I wanted to leap up and wave my arms around and scream to my stepfather, "It's all an act! Don't let her fool you!"

When I wasn't in school, I spent most of my time playing with dolls and writing about the habitually gray English weather. It was the kind of weather that created depressing fantasies, and I wrote stories about the sad, cold, homeless puppies of England who I imagined were unable to find food or shelter. Sometimes, when the weather permitted, we went to the Thames to feed the ducks. Other times I picked blackberries in the backyard. Mostly I played alone, in my own little world of dreams. I felt plucked and cut at the stem, like I was mourning something.

Then my mother became pregnant with Sara, and things grew more distant between us. It wasn't like she was ever consistently lighthearted, but she used to have her moments with me, like when we danced, and those moments were now reserved for her new husband and new baby.

After Sara was born, my mother became angrier with my grandmother and me. It felt like we could never do anything right. Whenever I entered a room where my mother was sitting, my grandmother would be walking out, her face drooping and saddened. Five minutes later, I would leave the room in a similar state. As a result, my grandmother and I spent a lot of time together. It was odd, how quiet the two of us had become, speaking in low tones to avoid upsetting my mother.

Sometimes I wondered if my mother wished to be completely rid of her past. Duty and responsibility had made her promise to care for her own mother and for her first daughter from an unsuccessful marriage, and she tried to make us a part of her new life. But often she couldn't hide her desire to separate from what had come before. Once, when we were having one of our fights, she told me she wished I was never born. I don't think what she said had anything to do with the fight; I think it was a moment of violent realization that she would never have a brand new start because her past was always there in front of her, in the form of her mother and first daughter.

By the time our family moved to the United States, to Los Angeles, when I was twelve, my grandmother and I were truly foreigners, both to our new country and also to my mother.

I woke up at noon on Christmas Day to the sound of yelling. Pulling myself out of bed, I staggered into the kitchen, where my mother and grandmother were cooking together and "just talking."

"Leave it alone!" my mother barked at my grandmother, who was trying to take a casserole dish out of the oven. She turned to me and frowned. "Rania, you sleep in so late, what's wrong with you?"

"There's nothing wrong with me."

"Well, get dressed," she mumbled, peeling some garlic.

"I am dressed," I said like a smartass.

She ignored me. "Where did I put the pepper?" she asked herself instead. She turned to rummage through the spice cabinet, found the pepper, and then let out a shriek when she saw her mother trying to take the dish out of the oven again. "Leave. It. Alone!"

"It's going to be too dry!" my grandmother groaned.

"I don't care if it's dry," my mother huffed. "It's my dish, my kitchen."

My grandmother wrung her hands and shook her head. From the other room, where Kyle, Sara, and Tiana were watching the Discovery Channel, the volume of the TV suddenly grew louder.

My stepfather, his hair still wet from the shower, stepped into the kitchen and announced that he was going to the store. He asked if my mother needed anything. She told him she needed bread.

"Okay," he said, turning to leave, but she stopped him, remembering she needed celery too.

"Okay, bread and celery," he said. "How much celery?"

"Put the sound down!" my mother hollered at the kids in the TV room. My grandmother slyly took this opportunity to retrieve the oven mitts.

"How much?" my stepfather asked again.

"What?" my mother asked, looking confused. "I said turn it down, Kyle!" she screamed.

"How much celery do you want?"

"I don't know, two bunches maybe."

My stepfather turned and left the kitchen.

"Oh no, wait!" she called. "Can you get me some asparagus too?"

"Did you say asparagus?" he asked from the other room.

My mother turned around to catch my grandmother once again lifting the plate out of the oven. "What are you doing?" she hollered as she ran to the oven.

"Asparagus?" came wafting from the other room.

"Put it back! I told you not to touch it!"

"You don't know what you're doing," my grandmother said, trying to wrestle the casserole dish away from her.

"Yes, I do! I do know what I'm doing!" my mother said, having won the fight over the casserole dish.

"Asparagus?"

"Leave it alone now!" she said sharply, slamming down the garlic press when she saw my grandmother fiddling with the knobs on the oven.

A ceramic bowl suddenly fell from the counter to the floor and broke.

"I've got it," I said, picking up the broken pieces.

"Asparagus?"

"Jesus, yes!" my mother screamed. "Asparagus, asparagus, asparagus!"

I attempted to sidestep out of the kitchen.

"Rania, I told you to get dressed!"

"Mom, Sara won't let me change the channel!" Kyle whined from the other room.

"Whatever, Kyle!" Sara hollered. Tiana began to cry.

"Sara, let him change the channel for a while."

"It's going to be too dry," my grandmother moaned dramatically.

"But I have to watch this for school!" Sara squealed.

"Uh-uh, no you don't, you liar!" Kyle retorted.

"Yes I do, Kyle!"

"How much?" my stepfather asked.

My mother put her hands up. "What?"

"Ow! Mom, Kyle pinched me!" Sara cried, and the sound of something breaking came from the TV room.

"Kyle!"

Tiana's crying turned to an outraged scream.

"Christ, Mom, pay attention for once. How much goddamn asparagus do you want?" I asked loudly.

"Don't talk to me that way!" she exclaimed.

Tiana ran into the kitchen, her face bright red. She stopped crying when she saw me, as if trying to remember who I was. Then, when a look of recognition crossed her face, she began wailing again. Kyle was now crying too, and he ran off to his room.

The front door slammed. My mother picked up Tiana, and my grandmother took over the garlic press, assuming my mother's responsibilities as if nothing had happened.

I slipped out of the kitchen as quietly as possible.

Later that night, I cornered my mother in the bathroom while she was getting ready for bed. I wanted to tell her about my dancing, and I'd not had the opportunity to talk to her alone since I'd arrived. I waited for the right moment, while she was smearing vitamin E oil over her face.

"I have to tell you something, Mom,"

"What?" she asked, giving me a glance in the mirror as she brushed her teeth.

"I just wanted to tell you about my new job. I'm dancing now."

"Dancing?" Toothpaste frothed from her mouth. She spat and rinsed. "What do you mean, dancing? What does that mean?"

"I mean, I'm dancing. Is it so necessary to elaborate? At a club, you know. Dancing. For money."

"You mean a stripper?" She patted her mouth dry with a towel; her face was unreadable.

"Yeah."

She bit a thumbnail thoughtfully. "Do you like it?"

"I like dancing on the stage."

She opened the medicine cabinet and rummaged through it. "You were always a very good dancer," she said, tossing a bottle of pills at me. "It's valerian-root capsules. It should help you sleep."

"Thanks." I didn't know she'd be so nonchalant. "Doesn't it bother you at all?"

"Why should it bother me?" she asked with irritation. "You're a grown woman. There's nothing wrong with what you do unless you feel there's something wrong."

"There's a lot of women I work with that don't tell their families,"

I said. "I've heard a couple of them say their parents disowned them or something."

My mother snorted. "That's very stupid. Do they think it's going to make them stop or something? Who is anyone to judge?"

I shrugged. My mother shook her head and yawned. "I have to go to bed."

She walked past me into her bedroom and closed the door. I stood alone in the hallway. The house was quiet. I got my journal and retreated to the patio.

Sitting there on the warm Christmas night, I wondered if my dancing really didn't bother her. In many ways, she was an open-minded woman, her liberal ways the result of being raised in exactly the same manner by her own mother. So she may truly have not been upset in the least. But I didn't know for sure because I was aware of the strength my mother carried, the same strength that her mother carried, the same strength they had handed down to me. The strength that taught me to repress my emotions, which forced them to lose their power, and thus helped to keep things in check. Though this was great for showing self-control, it did not lend itself to any kind of softness or warmth. It's what I grappled with every day; the softness inside with no outlet, because its roots were so elusive.

twelve

Returning to work was difficult. Onstage I felt like my body had forgotten how to dance, like I didn't really mean it anymore, like I didn't really mean to bend down, get on all fours, and crawl around like a sex-crazed creature, didn't really mean to twirl, twist, or gaze longingly into the eyes of men. My body felt rigid in its responses. Or maybe it was just getting sick of what it had to do.

Hoping to change things, I cut down on my drinking, limiting myself to one glass of wine a night. I also considered leaving for a new club. But the only other ones I knew of were nude clubs with lap dancing, and the other dancers I worked with had painted a dark picture of these places, leaving me with images of women with dripping genitalia rubbing up and down on men's crotches.

One night Yvonne invited me to go dancing with her at an after-hours club downtown. The place was smoky and dark, the usual, a bunch of rave kids bouncing around, clutching bottled water. The music's repetitive thumping immediately grated on my nerves, so

Egyptian Exotica

I told Yvonne I was taking a cab home. But she grabbed my arm and pulled me over to the bar where Charlie, the head of security at Ruby's, and another man in his mid-thirties, extremely clean-cut and well dressed, were sitting.

"Hey, guys!" she yelled, waving frantically. Charlie beckoned us closer. He said something that I couldn't make out into Yvonne's ear. She whispered back to him and he nodded. She turned and looked at me, looked back to Charlie, then to the man at his side.

"Do you want to make a little money tonight?" she screamed into my ear.

"Doing what?" I asked.

"Dancing, what else?"

"Here?"

She motioned with a hand, meaning outside the club. I shrugged. She smiled and gave Charlie and his friend a thumbs-up.

Before we left, Charlie gave us each a hit of Ecstasy. I had only taken Ecstasy once before, on a date with some guy. The drug did nothing for me, but the guy ended up telling me how much he loved me, then projectile vomiting. Charlie insisted that what he had was pure, absolutely pure, and that nothing bad would happen to us.

We drove to a house in Pacific Heights (which Jack used to call Specific Whites). On the way, Yvonne told me the clean-cut guy's name was Peter, and that she'd danced for him several times at Ruby's. She said he was a good customer, a good tipper.

"This is his house. He's a doctor ... a single doctor!" She smiled.

"Living out in the Midwest for now."

We parked in front of one of the many large, pristine houses lining the block. Yvonne told me we didn't need to stay too long, and all we had to do was dance a little. We'd make a killing—Peter was loaded.

Inside Peter's house, hardwood floors gleamed, reflecting the light of overhead chandeliers, and a set of large French doors led out to a tiny brick patio complete with a few wrought iron chairs and a small jasmine tree.

Peter politely asked if we cared for a drink, then invited us into the den, which held a large-screen television and a sleek stereo housed in an oak entertainment system. A bar sat in the corner of the room, and Peter made the drinks while Charlie fiddled with the stereo.

We sat on a fluffy tan couch, listening to music and drinking. Then Yvonne got up and began to massage Peter's shoulders and neck. At the same time, Charlie cut through a pile of cocaine with a MasterCard on the glass coffee table. He passed a rolled twenty-dollar bill around when he was done, and then became extremely annoyed with me when I tried to make a cocoa puff.

"What the fuck you doing?" he admonished in his thick Vietnamese accent. "That's good fucking coke, pure shit, you don't put that in a cigarette.." He grabbed the bill from my hand and did a line to prove a point. "See?" He rubbed his nose frantically. "It's the best. You have to enjoy it like good wine or cigar."

I told him it was more like a steak and that I got to decide how I wanted it cooked. He made a face and shook his head. I twisted the cigarette paper until the tobacco dropped, scooped up a little coke, mixed it up, then stuffed it back in and smoked it. I settled back down onto the couch, drank my Jack and Coke, and watched Peter and Yvonne whisper to each other like shy kids with secret crushes. When it was time to dance, we went upstairs to the bathroom to put on our costumes.

I looked at myself in the wide, spotless mirror. Being at a stranger's house in my stripper outfit was odd. I looked at Yvonne; in a black velvet evening gown and opera-length gloves, with small, tasteful, sparkling jewelry on her ears and wrist, she looked like she was on her way to a ball.

I self-consciously picked at my low-cut, high-slit silver dress and listened as she gushed about Peter. He was a catch. And cute, didn't I think so? And he was rich too. He wanted a girlfriend bad, couldn't I tell? He looked like he needed a wife, didn't I think so?

I sniffed the air. "Yvonne, it smells like potpourri in here. Are you sure he's straight?"

"Will you stop? You're freaking me out," she said, checking her face.

"Wouldn't it be weird to be his girlfriend?"

"Why would it be weird?" she asked. "He's sweet, he's nice, and he's got money and doesn't know what to do with it. You can't use your sexuality as a scapegoat to avoid involvement. You've got to take it where you can get it." She picked up a brush and started brushing her hair.

My mother always urged me to marry a man with money, a man who would take care of me. And the quieter he was, the fewer questions he asked, the better. Since I was never the settling-down type, this advice seemed a bit boring and generic to me. But Yvonne was the kind of woman my mother would call smart. She had that calculating precision that extremely successful strippers possess, a natural ball-breaking hardness that enables them to know exactly what they want and how to go out and get it, without allowing feelings to get in the way. I thought my feelings never got in the way. Obviously I was wrong.

"How ethical is it to get involved with somebody you dance for?" I asked.

Yvonne rolled her eyes and shook her head. "Ethical? I think you're missing the point. What's the purpose of dancing if it's not to make money?"

"I just like dancing," I said. It sounded so naïve.

"Well, that's fine," she responded. "But the work you do isn't only on the stage; most of it is done on the floor, or in the VIP room, or here. You can't tell me that you got into dancing only to be on the stage, because then you should be an actress instead." She picked a piece of lint off her dress.

"It's all about what you can make out of being in this business," she went on. "I see it as an opportunity, and I can choose to just make it a job or I can make it a real career, because it's something I'm good at. You wouldn't believe how many eligible guys are in the club and how many of them are looking for girlfriends, and they're willing to accept what you do for a living." She opened a tube of gloss, leaned into the mirror, and slid some more color onto her lips.

"Right. And they wouldn't go to strip clubs after you land them, is that it?" I spat back.

"You really do think too much," she said with a small smile. "You should enjoy tonight; we don't get many opportunities like this, you know."

We took turns dancing for Peter, who was getting pretty high and drunk. Charlie had brought enough cocaine to make us all overdose, and he kept snorting a line every few minutes. At some point, Yvonne took off Peter's pants, stripping him down to his boxers. Meanwhile, I downed several drinks and did more coke than I cared to, as Charlie gabbed to me about how he was in the Vietnamese mafia and other things I tried to ignore.

"Hey, Layla," he said to me. "Do you have a boyfriend?"

"No."

"Do you want one?"

"No."

"Why not?" he asked, pressing his thumb against his nose.

"What's the point, Charlie?" I snapped. "Who cares if I've got a boyfriend? When the hell are we getting paid?"

Yvonne looked over at me, widened her eyes, and mouthed the word Don't. Charlie settled back into his chair, hands clasped behind his head. "Hey, you know I'm waiting for some dances, too," he said, "We'll talk money later."

"Why not now? You know how we work it in the club."

"Hey, I'm a generous fucking man, you know, and I got money. You don't trust me?"

"I didn't say that," I told him, and Yvonne looked desperate now, looking from me to Peter while she continuing dancing.

"No? Look." He pulled an enormously fat wad of bills from his pocket, slipped them out of a gold money clip, and handed them to me. "Here, you hold it, I don't fucking care!" He rubbed his nose as his mouth twitched uncontrollably.

I grabbed the money and stuffed it into the front of my bra. Then I excused myself to go to the bathroom. Yvonne ran after me, saying she needed to freshen up. I shut the bathroom door behind us, then sank to the floor.

"Why did you do that?" she asked, irked. "They're going to pay us. He's got a lot of money."

"Look, we've been here three hours already, and this isn't business anymore," I said, throwing her a nasty look.

"It is business. You may not see it, but that's what's going on."

"God," I said. Her act seemed so transparent to me.

"What's your problem?" Yvonne snapped. "I'm doing you a huge favor and teaching you how to get a regular by bringing you here, and all you do is complain."

"Seems like a real pain in the ass," I mumbled.

"It isn't, once you get used to it," she assured me.

"I'm not sure I want to."

She shook her head, then greedily watched as I pulled the wad of money out from my dress and counted it. "How much? How much?" she kept asking, kneeling down next to me on the fluffy white bath mat.

"Eighteen hundred," I told her. "I don't know how anyone can be this stupid, carrying around this kind of cash." Yvonne nagged me to keep the money out of Charlie's sight.

"All right," I said. "Let's just get this over with and get the hell out of here."

Downstairs, I resisted Charlie's increasingly aggressive invitations to head into the bedroom as Yvonne began kissing Peter long and hard. After a few minutes, she pulled away, her lipstick smeared, a triumphant smile on her face. She'd done what she came to do, and now it was time to go. And it was about time too—it was daylight outside, and my knees were wobbling from the combination of drugs and exhaustion.

We headed upstairs, gathered our belongings into our bags in the bathroom, got dressed, and then headed back downstairs. When we got to the dining room, Charlie was looking around, glassy-eyed, his jaw twitching. Peter looked like he was about to pass out.

"Where are you guys fucking going?" Charlie demanded. Yvonne mumbled that it was time for us to go home.

"Home? But what about partying? Aren't we going to party? Why don't you and Peter go upstairs? And Layla, you come upstairs with me."

"No way," I said, grabbing the front-door knob. Charlie slammed the door shut before I could fully open it.

"What the fuck you mean, no way? You haven't done shit," he shouted, patting the breast of his jacket.

"I'm not fucking you," I informed him. "I'm not fucking anyone."

"You haven't done shit, okay? And you took my fucking money, too, so now you fucking stay." Yvonne went over and whispered something into his ear. "No fuck next time, you fucking whore, there isn't no fucking next time, are you fucking crazy? You promised, and you promised tonight."

"Promised what?" I asked Yvonne. She looked away from my gaze.

"Hey, buddy," Peter dragged himself off the sofa and patted Charlie on the shoulder. "It's okay, really, I had a good time, it's no big deal." Charlie knocked Peter's hand off his shoulder and patted his jacket again. Then his hand disappeared into it, and when it came out, it was holding a gun.

I didn't know anything about guns except that some were big, some were small, and all had a barrel and a trigger. Charlie's gun was small and black, and I looked into the barrel that was aimed at my face.

"You give me my fucking money now, okay?" Spittle formed at the corners of his mouth, and his hands shook. He looked like he was about to cry. "Otherwise your pretty brains are going to be all over this nice fucking floor."

"Charlie," Peter whimpered in a freaked-out voice. "Charlie, come on, man."

"Charlie," Yvonne's practical voice chimed in.

"Fuck you! Fuck you both!" Charlie screamed through clenched teeth.

Peter and Yvonne stood still where they were, waiting. I opened my mouth, but no sound came out. An eternity passed, and the world turned silent and still, with only the strange, empty sound of Charlie's now audible sobbing. Then, everything suddenly sped up as Yvonne and Peter lunged together toward Charlie, who violently jerked away from them, keeping the barrel aimed at my face.

"Give me the fucking money," he demanded again, harshly wiping the tears from his face.

My hands slowly dropped into my my jeans pocket, where I held the wad of cash. I took out the money and handed it to Charlie. He snatched it away, then lowered the gun. My breath shot out like I'd been underwater for too long. Peter grabbed the gun from Charlie's hands, and Yvonne and I ran out the front door. From inside the house I could hear Charlie's voice screaming, "You whores! You fucking whores!"

We drove in silence for a long time, until I put a hand under my jacket and took out the remaining money.

"Holy shit, you kept some of it?" she screamed.

My fingers shook as I counted.

"How much did you manage to get?"

It was a bright, cold day; the sun's glare was more than I could handle. "Eight hundred," I said, shielding my eyes with my hand.

"Hey, not bad," she said.

"What did you promise them?" I asked.

She didn't answer, just stared into the windshield like she was weighing her words. In the end, she told me nothing, and she didn't need to.

thirteen

A week later, I quit working at Ruby's. I didn't bother telling Tony because, well, what was the point? Dancers changed clubs all the time—there was no notice to give, we just walked out and didn't come back, and someone quickly filled our spot because the industry was a revolving door that never stopped spinning, and we were all replaceable.

Since I was fed up with the world of upscale clubs and their bullshit designed to make things seem glamorous, I decided to venture in a new direction—nude lap dancing. Though I'd heard much bad-mouthing about this kind of dancing from the other women at Ruby's (Tony thought it was the gutter of the stripping world), the upscale clubs looked to me like a government full of promises and ideals, with rampant corruption festering beneath the polished, gleaming surface. So I figured that whatever I was heading into couldn't be much worse.

Having no particular club in mind, I decided to wander the city one day in search of my next dancing destination. I started out near

Market and Seventh, where I knew of a few places, but quickly decided that any club next to a check-cashing place seemed too sketchy for me.

I headed from Market Street to Powell, then to Union Square, where I had seen Tony Bennett, clad in turquoise pants and a bright yellow sports jacket, give a free concert on my twenty-first birthday. I turned left, walked a little farther, and then collapsed onto a bus-stop bench. I was exhausted; it was cold and damp, and I hadn't had the courage to enter a single club. I decided to give up for the day and wait for the bus to take me home.

When I first came to San Francisco, I worked as a waitress in a little café on the second floor of the Center for the Arts, next to the Moscone Convention Center. There I served snobby lunches to snobby people: salads of velvety edible flowers drizzled with anise-infused vinaigrettes, always with a side of chutney, because everyone wanted a side of chutney. When my shift was over, I would walk up Market Street in order to familiarize myself with the area, usually ending up at the Ellis bus station, where I was now. As I waited for the bus, my eyes were always drawn to the cheesy, flashing neon leg, bent up in a cancan stance, in front of Gigi's.

I stood when the bus pulled up, but instead of getting on, I stepped away. The driver gave me a dirty look, then closed the door.

Gigi's may have been a hole in the wall, but at least it was a clean, cute hole in the wall. Dimly lit with pink, red, and yellow lights, the moderately sized room was filled with small cocktail tables surrounded by folding chairs; the center of each table held a fat, red blazing candle. In the corner, cushioned with black vinyl, sat a low-key bar that did not serve alcohol, as liquor and nudity, by law, did not mix in California. The place felt more like a local neighborhood joint than a nude club.

The dancers, wearing bikinis or bras and G-strings, hung out together in a booth next to the bar. Near them, at the corner of the small stage, sat a red heart-shaped basket. When a dancer was done with her set, another dancer plucked the basket off the stage and went around the room with a smile, collecting tips for her.

"Have you been dancing long?" asked Sally, the manager, a woman in her forties with clumpy mascara.

"About a year," I said. "But not lap dancing."

"Well, don't worry about it too much, honey. I'll have some of the girls show you what it's all about. The girls here are really nice, and they all have their own way of doing their dances, so you'll work on it until you find something you're comfortable with."

"Okay," I said, surprised; no manager in a strip club, save for Mike, had ever spoken so kindly or sincerely to me before.

We walked to a hallway in the back of the club, where little booths were sectioned off with black drapes. Sally explained that this was where the lap dances took place. Each booth was furnished with a chair and a small lamp that glowed a dim orange.

"You close the curtain when you dance, and make sure you open it when you're done," she said.

"How much are the dances?" I asked.

"There's no set price. There's a thirty-dollar fee per night for you to use the space. All I ask is that you pay it by ten o'clock every time you work, and that you don't do anything illegal or nasty in the booths, because lap dances are all the girls do here."

"Really," I said, shocked that there was no set price.

"We don't charge you a percentage from your dances," she went on, "so you can charge whatever you'd like. I'd talk to the girls first if I were you, to see what they're charging, just to make sure you're all doing the dances for about the same price. I think it's twenty dollars these days."

"Do dancers always collect tips for each other in that little basket?" I asked.

"That's right," Sally said with a smile. "I like to make sure everyone gets paid, and I think it encourages my girls to be considerate of each other."

"That's a really good idea," I said, impressed.

She laughed and looked at me. "I'm glad you like it. Does that mean you'd like to work here?"

I nodded and she said she was glad. She put her hand on my back and led me over to the bar area to put together a weekly schedule.

Feeling good, I went home and thought about the differences between Gigi's and the other two places I'd danced at. Gigi's didn't charge for dances, didn't charge for anything but the space itself. There wasn't even a deejay, just a jukebox in the dressing room, preloaded with money and ready to play whatever song you wanted. At Glitterati's and Ruby's, I had been paying to work there, paying a hell of a lot to work there. In addition to taking my money, they gave me rules to follow, and I had to pay even more money if I broke any of those rules. It was like paying for a new car, then being charged each time I drove it. I'd thought all clubs charged these fees and had their stupid little rules, but after speaking to Sally, I saw that this was not true. I began to realize that the whole deal at Glitterati's and Ruby's was about the club lining its pockets at the expense of the dancers. I thought of all the nights I'd walked out empty-handed or, worse, owing money. I remembered being nagged and threatened by the managers to pay up, to start making some money or else, and I'd been so worried, so anxious, because I had nothing to give. Talk about "upscale"; it was upscale pimping. The club took from the dancers and, in fact, made most of its money from the dancers, yet it was the dancers that kept the club open. The attitude of the two clubs I'd worked in—and I was sure now that the rest of the upscale places were the same—told me that though the sex industry needed women, it was in fact contemptuous of this need. It was like much of the general male population, which wanted women on such a base level, yet hated them at the same time for bringing out those base feelings. In the end, the men and the clubs got what they needed, which they didn't want to admit they needed, and the women were punished for providing that need.

fourteen

I refused to dance completely nude during my first couple weeks at Gigi's and instead wore underwear while onstage. Rather than being angry that I was covering up what they had come to see, the customers seemed fascinated by my "shyness" and tried coaxing me into total nudity with larger and larger tips. I capitalized on this for as long as I could, until the other dancers began giving me suspicious looks.

Intimidated into nudity, I danced nervously in my black stilettos and black fishnet thigh-highs, a rhinestone choker around my neck, acutely aware of the men's eyes on the one area of myself I had never exposed onstage. In order to offer the clientele an unobstructed view, I had shaven myself clean, leaving a little gratuitous patch on top that looked like Hitler's moustache.

I quickly got used to the total nudity but still wouldn't approach men for lap dances because I didn't know how and, frankly, I was not enthusiastic about learning. One evening, I announced my ignorance in the dressing room. Upon hearing this, one of the other dancers, a big woman named Katiya with cropped purple hair, ordered me to "sit down." I complied, and she immediately climbed on top of me, grabbed the back of the chair with both hands, and, to the rhythm of the music coming from the next room, began to gyrate her pelvis into my face.

"You just wiggle around, rub up against them like that, back and forth," she said in synchronicity with the pulse of the music. I could hardly breathe with her large body pressed on top of me.

"Ugh!" another dancer named Amber exclaimed. She was a tidy-looking, petite little woman, with every hair in place. "I can't believe you do it like that. Do you know how easy it would be for them to lick you?" She walked over, motioned for Katiya to move aside, then positioned herself between my legs. "I just use my knee, it's less of a problem, you know. They can't do anything," she said, caressing my pelvic bone with her bare knee before turning around and wiggling her ass in my face, then bringing it down lightly into my lap. "A lot of girls do it this way," she said.

"Yeah, I do it that way, too," another dancer, Divine, said as she watched us in the mirror while brushing her hair. She was serious-looking and always wore black velvet corsets. "But you've got to be careful, or they'll grab you if you're not looking."

"They grab?" I asked nervously.

"It hardly ever happens," Divine said with a shrug. "But sometimes . . ."

"There's always an asshole," Haley, a perky blonde, said from a chair across the room.

"If you straddle, you get more control," Katiya interrupted, smoothing her eyebrows with a fingertip. "All your weight is on them, and they can't really get away with anything. Plus, the guys really like it."

"It depends on the guy," Haley interjected. "Most of them are pretty nice here, all regulars, you know, so they're not jerks or anything."

"We do have a few weirdo regulars," Divine assured me.

"Yeah, I had the smelly Indian guy last week," Katiya remembered.

"That guy that smells like rotten tacos?" Haley said, wrinkling her nose.

"Yeah, and onions," Amber chimed in. "He likes to come in here when he hasn't showered."

"God, he's so gross," Haley shuddered dramatically. "And he's all handsy too."

"I mean, it's bound to happen anywhere, at any club, the grabbing," Katiya told me. "But nobody ever gets too weird."

"And it's easy to put 'em in their place when they start screwing around," Divine added, still brushing her hair.

They all went quiet for a moment, until Amber asked, "So, are you still scared or what?"

The next night, after I finished my set, I returned to the floor, determined to do my first lap dance. I didn't have to ask, however; an extremely fat man with dark hair and a dark fuzzy beard approached me.

"Hi there," he said with a wide smile. "I'm Jim, are you new?"

"Layla," I said, shaking his great paw. "Yeah, I'm new, just started."

"Wonderful," he said excitedly, and with great formality added, "May I be one of the first to have the honor of escorting you back to the lovely booths?" As we walked to the booths, I wondered, in a panic, how I was going to dance for him; he was so fat.

I closed the drapes behind me, then nervously bit my lip as he sunk down slowly as a sunset into the seat, which disappeared beneath his enormous backside.

"Well then," he said amiably. "When I'm here, I usually like to be straddled by the dancer, because I find it a little more intimate."

"Okay," I said, thrown off by his directness. I watched as he reached into the back pocket of his jeans and produced his wallet, which was connected to his belt loop with a chain. He thumbed through some bills and pulled out a fifty, handing it to me.

"Will this be enough for your trouble?" he asked, closing his wallet and putting it back in his pocket.

"Yes," I responded.

"Wonderful," he said with a smile. He then looked at me expectantly. Not wanting to look like I was spending too much time trying to figure things out, I did a kind of tackling-lunge and straddled him.

"Very good," he said. "I like your approach."

I giggled weakly.

"I like very petite exotic women," he told me. "Usually I get dances from Amber, and there was also another girl called Rain, though she doesn't come in here too much anymore." As he talked, I tried to gyrate and give at least a semblance of a lap dance. But it wasn't working because he was too big, and I could only reach his belly.

After a few minutes of my pointless squirming, he told me that he usually just liked to talk to the dancer while she straddled him. Relieved, I put my arms around his thick neck and sat on him. It was like being on Santa's lap (maybe that was his fantasy?), and we made small talk until his time was up.

To my surprise, the lap dances didn't bother me as much as I thought they would. I think the reason for this was that the needs of the men that came into Gigi's were very different from those of the men who came into the upscale topless clubs. The men at Gigi's wanted actual closeness; they wanted to touch my hair, my face, and a lap dance was only good for them if I gave the signal that I was genuinely interested, not simply trying to make a buck. Many of them were lonely, looking for a girlfriend, a friend, or simply someone to briefly touch and talk to.

The men at Glitterati's and Ruby's also wanted the dancer to be interested, but it was on a glitzier, flashier level, and the more glamorous-looking the woman, the better. The general sentiment was "look at what I've got." As a dancer, I found it easier to deal with a man's loneliness than with the elusive, frivolous charm and talk of the upscale topless world. It was less trying, and more honest, to respond with kindness and empathy than with false glamour and a programmed smile.

I also acquired my first admirer at Gigi's: A tall, lanky man, with drooping shoulders and a bad haircut began sending me roses and chocolates. I'd only done one dance for him, and he didn't say much, only grinned at me adoringly, which I usually interpreted as a happy erection. But now I stood in the dressing room holding another gold box filled with roses and a card that read, "To the most beautiful dancer at Gigi's, from your secret admirer." (Well, not so secret: I had seen him slip the box into Katiya's hands a few minutes earlier.)

Divine and Haley peeked over my shoulder to read the card, then exploded into peals of laughter.

"Ooh my God, she's got Barry," Haley squeaked.

"Oh, Barry, Barry, Barry," Divine shook her head and sighed dramatically.

"Did you say Barry?" Amber piped in.

"Sweetie," Divine said, "one of the most wonderful things is about to happen to you."

"What?" I asked, having abandoned the gold box as I slipped into a new dress.

They started laughing again, and then Divine explained.

"You've just landed the easiest money in the world, and all you have to do is ask for it."

"There's a catch, right?" I responded, fumbling around for my thigh-highs. Divine shook her head, her blunt-cut blue-black hair slicing across her face.

"No catch. Just imagine a guy with no life and more money than he knows what to do with, then combine that with zero social skills and bad self-esteem, and what do you have?"

"Barry!" rose in unison from everyone in the dressing room.

"He'll send you the standard roses and chocolates for a while," Divine went on, "then he'll tell you he's in love with you."

"Then he'll want to take you out," Haley giggled. "On a date."

"But trust me," Divine said steadily. "The best thing you can do is go shopping."

"Shopping?"

"He doesn't do cash gifts," Haley said.

"Thinks it's too impersonal," Divine explained. "I've had him, and let me tell you, the best thing to do is go to Piedmont." I nodded, remembering the outrageously priced costume shop off Haight Street with the drag-queen salesgirls. "Take him there in the afternoon, and buy yourself some stuff. He'll pay for it."

"What do you mean, he'll pay for it?"

"Okay, listen," Haley said. "I had him too, and it's like this: He asks you out, and then you go, 'Oooh, I'd love to go out, Barry, but maybe we can meet at Piedmont before we do anything, because I really need some new stuff for work.' And he'll be all, 'Well, I don't know,' and you say, 'Well, sweetie, I'm really busy but I want to see you, don't you want to see me?' And then you pout, and eventually he'll just do it because he's got no spine. And then you go in there with him, and the drag queens that work there all know him, so they'll start bringing out the most expensive stuff. And then you do a little fashion show for him, trying on everything. You can get him to spend fifteen hundred easy, maybe even more."

"It's so easy," Divine said.

"I can't do that!" I exclaimed, but they all insisted that I could, and I should.

Egyptian Exotica

Maybe I was not confident enough to do it, or maybe I simply didn't feel right hustling some poor guy, no matter how quickly and how often he fell in love with a dancer.

In the end, I avoided Barry. Part of me felt good for not taking his money, while another part of me wondered what good it was to do this kind of work if I was going to turn down opportunities for making money, easy money.

fifteen

In the early summer, I planned a two-week trip to New Orleans with Katiya and another dancer named Savannah. The trip was ostensibly for pleasure, but I brought some dancing outfits along, just in case I wanted to make a little extra money. Divine said New Orleans boasted some of the most interesting clubs in the country.

We landed at a guesthouse in the Garden District at about midnight, the tropical heat slipping through my body like I was translucent. At the front desk, a heavy-lidded, blond, pink-skinned guy stood nursing a can of Keystone beer. He introduced himself as Rick, checked us in, took our money, and told us that coffee and doughnuts were served daily from seven to ten in the morning. Then he slowly led us down a hallway, lined with muted yellow wallpaper covered with a print of tiny sparrows alighting on leaves and branches, toward a wooden staircase that led upstairs.

"We got air-conditioning in all the rooms," he said as we went up. "And we do maid service whenever you want, so if you need anything, just ask." I watched the back of his pink freckled legs bend as he moved up the staircase, his soft white and pink feet encased in thick sandals.

"Do you have maps?" Savannah asked. Rick said he had some downstairs behind the desk.

We made our way down a stuffy hallway, past a few closed doors, until we reached our room. Rick opened the door, and we were immediately hit in the face with a slap of icy air from a powerful air conditioner. He flipped on the light by the door, revealing a modestly sized room with a shabby queen-size bed pushed against one wall, a bunk bed pressed against the other. The blasts from the air conditioner made the short, flimsy yellow curtains spastically shake and dance. Rick walked into the room and pushed open another door in the corner near the bunk bed. The bathroom.

"We got more soap downstairs, too," he said. "And if you need towels—"

"I've got my own," Savannah said primly. She was a no-nonsense woman who didn't smile often and always wore her long hair in fastidious braids that hung over her large, matronly bosom. I followed her inside the bathroom, while Katiya inspected the closet.

The bathroom was small and smelled like bleach. The bathtub was caked with hard-water stains, with a ring of orange rust around the faucet. Lying in the tub, almost dead, its legs still kicking away faintly, was a king-size cockroach. I screamed at the top of my lungs.

"Is the place infested?" Savannah shouted at Rick.

"Look," he said with a smile. "It's summer and we get a lot of bugs in the city."

"Is there a problem here, in this room?" I demanded. "Are they going to crawl on me while I sleep?"

"Look," Rick said impatiently, "it's not like an infestation, you know, they're summer creatures, man, they come in when they see the light and . . ."

I left the bathroom before he finished his sentence and sat on the slightly sunken, exceedingly squishy bed. Katiya flopped down beside me and put an arm over my shoulder. Then I heard the toilet flush, and Rick and Savannah came out of the bathroom.

"There, I flushed it down the toilet. It's all gone now," he said with a half-smile. He gave Savannah three sets of keys, then left. She shut the door behind him, then started fiddling with her bra strap. I looked out the corner of my eye and noticed my black spiked dancing heel sticking out of my half-zipped suitcase. It was an odd thing to see, like something that had followed me from another dimension, a reminder (or an invitation). Despite bringing my stripping clothes, I really didn't want to dance while on vacation if I could help it.

Exhausted, we immediately went to sleep, Katiya in the top bunk, Savannah and I sharing the bed. Lying there in the dark, I felt like something was biting me. After a few minutes of tossing and turning, I sat up and turned on the light. Savannah and Katiya simultaneously groaned in displeasure.

"Sorry," I said, searching the sheets. "I feel like something is biting me."

"It's just the mosquitoes," Savannah said, but I didn't believe her. Wouldn't I be able to hear them buzzing around?

"It's the prickly heat," Katiya suggested groggily.

"Isn't that only in dry and hot places, like Arizona?" Neither one responded.

Done with my search, I turned off the light. Instead of falling asleep, though, I tossed and turned some more, until Savannah sighed loudly to shut me up. Trying to remain still, I tucked my face into the scratchy fabric of the sheets, smelling the cheap detergent. I snuggled into the covers and squeezed my eyes shut, trying to relax. Only when the sky began to lighten with the dawn did I pass out in exhaustion.

I woke up to the sounds of Katiya and Savannah arguing.

"Screw the swamps!" Katiya exclaimed. "I'm from Florida, I can see them anytime!"

"Then I'll go alone!" Savannah snapped. She looked at me. "Do you want to go to the swamps?"

"I have family in Florida."

"Fine." She left the room and slammed the door hard.

"What the hell is her problem?" I asked, my brain still packed in sleep.

"She's got some stupid list of things she wants to do, tourist stuff," Katiya sighed.

"What time is it?" I mumbled, looking around. The sun was peeking through the yellow curtains. I tried to shield my eyes from its brightness.

"Noon," Katiya said. "We've been up for a couple hours, but you were passed out hard, so we just let you sleep."

We spent most of the day in the French Quarter soaking up the heat and margaritas. The humidity was dizzying, and we stopped every few minutes at a different bar for a fresh drink. Little black children, looking cool despite the heat, tap-danced on the sidewalks, bottle caps stuck to the bottom of their shoes. Eventually, we hit Bourbon Street, where Katiya stopped to eye the strip clubs. I used that as an opportunity to separate from her.

"I'll meet you back at the guesthouse."

I ambled around the Quarter some more, then headed back to the Garden District, the stinky hot air filling my nostrils. After wandering for a few hours, I stopped at a coffee shop and began scribbling in my journal, the words coming quickly, my hand struggling to keep up. Usually when I wrote, it was the other way round, my pen moving, the thoughts following, like a wooden spoon in some great cauldron trying to thicken a pitifully thin stew. But here in New Orleans, my thoughts were on overdrive, like blood spilled on some great sacrificial altar.

I returned to the guesthouse as night set in. But the sky didn't darken fully into an inky black here, instead remaining a hazy orange or plum while the moon hung like a grotesquely large yet beautifully ripe fruit.

I spent the rest of my vacation exploring New Orleans, and I liked what I saw. I found the dilapidation of the city appealing. In a vague way I couldn't finger, it reminded me of Egypt, Alexandria in particular. I was strangely exhilarated by the crumbling splendor of the past mixed with the obnoxious tourism of the present.

Egyptian Exotica

The town was like a decrepit museum filled with the artifacts of gambling, drinking, and stripping. It was an odd city, but I was an odd person, and I was drawn to the strange contradictions that made New Orleans what it was, whatever that was. Besides, I was bored with San Francisco and sick of the cold night fog, of sitting on the back porch of my flat, trying to write and make sense out of everything, which never seemed to happen. I thought it might be time for a change of scenery.

I decided to extend my stay, but to do that I needed some extra cash. Katiya and Savannah suggested I try Milady's Quarter's. It was a cheesy little upscale place with a plastic jungle setting, fake palm trees, and four tiny stages. I got hired, then left in a huff a few hours later when I found out I couldn't do any floor work. There were times when I liked to crawl around on all fours, like a cat in heat. It was my way of dancing, yet Milady's didn't allow it, and I suddenly remembered why I had stopped working at upscale strip clubs in the first place.

Later that night, I returned to the guesthouse and discovered that I had a nasty case of poison ivy, which I'd caught from sharing the bed with Savannah. It was all because of her goddamn swamp expeditions. At first we thought they were mosquito bites, and we slathered citronella oil over the bumps, which only made things significantly worse. Even if I did want to stay in New Orleans, I couldn't dance for the time being because I looked like a red-spotted freak.

Before I left to go back to San Francisco, I mentioned to Rick my plans for relocation. He told me that when and if I decided to come,

Rania Zada

I could stay at the guesthouse free of charge until I found a place of my own. All I needed to do for my room and board was work a few hours a week answering phones and checking in tourists. I watched him guzzling a can of Keystone, as he'd been doing every time I'd seen him for the past two weeks. Perhaps, I thought, he needed the extra time away from his "responsibilities" to drink himself into oblivion.

sixteen

Upon returning, I immediately noticed a disturbing change at Gigi's. Several new dancers had been hired, many of them quite skanky. Among the highlights, or lowlights: Elaine, who was pushing fifty and whose main bit was dancing to Prince's "Soft and Wet," then sitting with her legs spread onstage, a spray bottle in hand, squirting water on her pussy as her mouth puckered in a glossy, porn "O." One night I walked by a booth and saw the back of her heels sticking out, and I noticed, when she returned to the dressing room a few minutes later, that bright red lipstick was smeared all over her face. It didn't take long to figure out what she'd been doing.

Then there was Silk, tall and lanky with long, straight, blunt-cut red hair, who did Elaine one better, as she supposedly had sex in the booths. Another new woman with a name I never learned tied her labia into a knot onstage. This was her entire act; she came on in a bikini, then fiddled herself senseless as she lay on the floor, her back against the mirror. I watched in fascination as she untied the knot and stretched the skin about five to six inches from her vagina, a look of smug satisfaction on her face. Before I left for vacation, Gigi's was a cute little dive; now it was gaining on seedy in weekly strides.

One night, at the end of a slow shift, my basket returned to the stage with an unusually large sum of money in it. Looking around in the darkness, I spotted Cindy, of all people, at a table in the back, along with an older man, whom I recognized as Phil, the regular from Glitterati's with a thing for blondes.

I made my way offstage, got dressed, then headed out to the main floor. Cindy, wearing a little pink summer dress and a faded denim jacket, sat next to Phil, who was wearing a no-nonsense black business suit. Both of them smiled widely when I approached.

"My God, where have you been?" Cindy squealed, grabbing my hand as though I were her long-lost best friend and not her foil from Edie's lesbian game.

"I just sort of decided to disappear," I replied.

"Well, you're not missing out on much," she sighed. "Ruby's is totally slow. Way too many girls work there now. It's a drag. It's smart of you to work here. This place totally has a little underground following. I always hear about it. By the way, have you ever met Phil?" Cindy's eyes widened as she introduced him.

"I remember you," he said with a smile and a wink, grabbing my hand and not letting go. Cindy squeezed my other hand, and both of them looked at me expectantly.

"Are you going home?" Cindy asked me. I told her I was probably going to have a drink at a bar called the Gold Dust.

"Do you mind if we join you?" Phil asked. "I'll pay you."

"To have a drink?"

"Just a drink," he assured me with a smile, producing some bills from his wallet. He slid them discreetly across the table. "A drink, in a bar."

"Well, I–"

"Great," he said. "We can meet you there in a few minutes, after you leave." He excused himself to go to the restroom. Cindy was still beaming at me.

"He likes you," she said.

"Is he your regular?"

"No, he takes me out once in a while, but he's not really my regular. We're friendly, and he helps me out with money a lot, and he likes to talk to me, but it's not like that. But I know he's looking."

"Oh really?" I asked, taking the money off the table, then counting it. Four hundred dollars! For a drink in a bar?

Cindy laughed. "He's been well trained. He always pays for your time, no matter what."

At the Gold Dust, I sat between the two of them at the bar, drinking red wine. Phil was mostly quiet, occasionally tapping his foot to the music and drumming his fingers on the bar. He turned to me often and smiled. There was a kindness in his face I liked, a serenity. Cindy kept touching my hair as she slugged down Amaretto sours, growing tipsier by the minute.

"It's getting so long," she murmured, running a hand over my hair. "It looks so great."

"Thanks," I said, lighting a cigarette, which she quickly pulled out of my hands and took a drag of, before feeding it back to my lips. Phil watched, one elbow propped up on the bar, his face resting in his hand. He reached over with his other hand and touched my hair. What's with couples and the hair thing? I wondered, remembering Candy and Carl.

"I hear you're from Egypt," he said.

I nodded.

"I didn't believe Cindy when she told me," he said, a serious look on his face, as though he were weighing something.

"What's so hard to believe?"

"I don't know," he said. "You just don't meet many that work in your field."

"Ah," I said. For some absurd reason men often didn't believe me when I told them where I was from. They thought I was lying, trying to play up the exotic thing. Little did they know that the exotic thing was not an easy sell, as my cultural background either excited customers or turned them off completely. There was never a happy medium. The ones it aroused, I wondered what they saw when they looked at me, what fantasy was I playing out for them? An exotic belly dancer from a faraway land? The conservative Muslim girl gone bad?

"I hated Layla for a long time because Edie had the hots for her," Cindy said, interrupting my thoughts.

"Whatever happened to her anyway?" I asked, trying to act nonchalant.

"She's dead," Cindy said flatly.

I put my wineglass down. "Dead?"

Cindy fumbled in her purse for a cigarette. "She's dead to me," she muttered, lighting her cigarette. "I don't know what the hell happened to her."

"Edie?" Phil joined in. "I remember her. Strange girl, intense."

"Did you know Layla's from Egypt?" Cindy chirped as she grabbed my arm.

Phil turned to me and smirked. We were on our second drinks, while Cindy was already on her fourth, in addition to whatever else she'd had earlier in the evening. The more she drank, the more she wiggled in her seat, the more her already short pink dress inched farther and farther up her thigh. At one point, an elderly man on his way to the bathroom passed by, saw her naked thigh flashing, and grinned with a wild twinkle in his eye.

"Hi," she said wickedly, winking at him. He stopped next to her, opened his mouth, then turned bright red and hurried away.

"Maybe we should get out of here," Phil observed.

We tried to help Cindy to her feet, but she almost toppled over before Phil threw his arm around her waist. I pulled her dress down.

Once outside in the cold air, she perked up a little and was able to stand on her own, though she was still swaying. We flagged down a cab and headed to Nob Hill to drop off Phil first, since his place was closest. When we pulled up to his street, he put his business card in my hand.

"Call me," he said, giving my hand a squeeze. "I'd love to talk to you again."

Then, looking at Cindy, he said with concern, "Take care of her, please," before closing the car door. Cindy gave him a drunken little wave, then turned back to the window and started to bite her nails, which she did for the rest of the ride. When we got to her apartment, she seemed shaky, and I asked if she needed help upstairs. She said she did.

"I'll be right back," I told the cab driver.

Cindy leaned on me as walked into her building, then went up the stairs to her apartment. When we got there, she unlocked the door and stood in the darkened hallway.

"C'mon in for a sec," she slurred. "I wanna show you my place."

"But—"

"Just for a second," she said. I hesitated but went in. She turned on the light. It was a beautiful single flat with hardwood floors, and a four-poster bed in the center of the room, perfectly made, with a white fluffy comforter, white fluffy pillows, and white chiffon draped over it. Very bridal suite, I thought.

"It's really nice," I assured her and then told her it was good seeing her again. As I walked toward the door, she began to sob quietly.

"What's wrong?" I asked.

"Can't we hang out and have a drink and talk?" she mumbled through her tears.

"It's late and I'm really tired, Cindy," I said.

She walked over and put her arms around me. "Stay the night with me!" she sobbed.

"You need some sleep," I said. "Drink some water, then go to sleep. You'll feel better tomorrow."

"No!' She squeezed me tightly, then moved her face closer to mine, trying to kiss me. I pulled away, and she lunged for me. Not knowing what else to do, I ran into the kitchen.

"I'll get you some water," I yelled.

I flipped on the light. The kitchen was spotless, like it'd never been used, the walls white and bright. I returned and tried to put the water glass in her hand, but she angrily knocked it away and it fell with a thud to the wooden floor.

"Fine," I said, then made for the front door.

"You're just like Edie!" she screamed at me as I left. "You just sit there and fuck with my head and then leave!"

I could still hear her screaming as I ran down the stairs.

Phil started coming into Gigi's on a regular basis to see me. I was always polite and sweet and listened to what he had to say, as I actually liked him. But when he started giving me that puppyish falling-for-you face, I became aware of the dangerous transaction that was taking place between us: I made him feel a certain way, and he paid me for that feeling. Onstage this was entertainment, but in the booths it was a gun loaded with intimacy. So, although I danced for him, I didn't hustle him, didn't bat my eyelashes, didn't ask him to stay longer, like a good stripper who wanted a regular would have done. Instead, I was the one who cut it off early, telling him I had to leave. Phil couldn't figure me out, but my behavior was interpreted as mysterious, which made me even more attractive to him. Men are notorious for romanticizing situations (and women) they know absolutely nothing about.

The other dancers saw what was going on. They knew what Phil was worth; Divine knew of him through other dancers from Glitterati's.

"I don't get why your little ass isn't back there milking him for all he's worth," she said, cornering me in the dressing room one night. "It's not like he can't afford it, and you're the only one in this dump he wants."

"Is he shy?" Haley asked.

"No, Layla's the one cutting it short."

The rest of the dancers looked at me like I was a moron.

"It just doesn't feel right," I protested weakly. "I don't want to rip him off."

"Then marry him," Divine snorted.

"I don't like him like that, he's a customer!"

"What, you think he doesn't know what this is all about?" Divine pressed. "You think he's some sacrificial fucking lamb at your mercy and you're sparing him?" She laughed. "Come on, honey, get serious!"

"She did the same thing with Barry," Haley realized.

"No shit, she thinks she's saving them."

"I do not."

"Um . . . they're here to spend money," Haley informed me.

"I know that!" I yelled. "I'm not opposed to taking the money. But it's different onstage than in the booths; I just don't like getting that close."

"No one says get close, just take the damn money and run if you don't want to date him."

"Men fucking make money all the time," Amber said. "Why shouldn't we make a good living?"

"That's not what this is about," I argued.

"Bullshit! We're just as smart, so why the hell should we stand there and act helpless and not go out and get all the things we need? That's what this is all about!"

"It is not," I insisted. "That's what you want to make it about."

"They deserve to have all their fucking money taken," Haley muttered to herself.

"No, they don't," I argued.

"You're way too nice, Layla," Divine said.

I felt myself growing more defensive. I'd never thought of myself as too nice, yet hearing the observation made me feel a small degree of shame.

"Does he want to date you?" Savannah asked.

"That's the other thing," I said. "Phil mentions flying here and there, and taking me places."

"Why don't you date him?" Amber frowned. "He's fucking perfect, girl."

"And he seems nice," Savannah added.

"He is nice!" I exclaimed.

"So what is your problem?" they all asked.

"I don't know," I said, looking down. "That kept-woman thing, I guess."

"Why is taking money at your job being a kept woman?"

Savannah asked defensively. "And what makes you think we aren't being fucking kept every night we work here?"

"That's not what I mean," I said. I'd turned all the strippers against me.

"Well, we're all kept a few hours a night by different men when we're here, aren't we?" she insisted.

"Not consistently," I whispered, but she was right: We were all kept, one song at a time, one hour, one year, whatever. And being a kept woman in such a business was the best kind of promotion. It's just that I didn't want to be promoted at all. That was thinking long-term in a business I had no desire to be in long-term. I wanted only to be happy on the stage, and to make others happy when they watched me. It was a naïvely simple desire, but it was how I felt. My outlook may have been unrealistic to some, but I couldn't get away from it, and I didn't even know if I wanted to.

A lot of dancers are bamboozled by the idea that if they are ballbusters, then they're as powerful as men. It's the "get even" thing. However, I couldn't take a man's money and then justify it by saying that the son of a bitch deserved it because he was a man and all men were goddamn pigs. Is this what it takes to make a woman feel empowered? She must throw away her essence, her compassion, her understanding and replace it with the same kind of narrow-minded, self-serving male behavior she's always complaining about? As far as I was concerned, if a man wasn't compassionate or understanding, then he was a son of a bitch and a goddamn pig, and I wasn't going to stoop to that level to prove anything to him, or to myself. I would've preferred to throw on a man's suit and stuff a rolled-up sock in my slacks; at least I knew that was fun.

And, aside from all that, for the most part, I actually liked men. Phil was genuinely nice and considerate, and it didn't seem right to take all his money and then run out of town without a word.

Maybe I was just a coward in a G-string after all.

I finally told Phil that I was leaving town and never coming back. He nodded solemnly, then mentioned visiting me.

"I don't want anything in my life to remind me of dancing," I told him. "I'm not going to dance anymore after I move." And though this was my plan, it still felt like a lie.

Without a word, Phil left Gigi's, and I never saw him again.

seventeen

The Mitchell Brothers O'Farrell Theatre gleamed in the distance, like an overflowing treasure chest. The O'Farrell Theatre, once home to Marilyn Chambers. The O'Farrell Theatre, San Francisco's most infamous strip club, where you could supposedly dance your way to thousand-dollar nights.

I had considered working there a few times but had never had the guts. The audition was a grueling affair. I had heard tales that if the other dancers didn't like you, they threw pennies at your head during the audition. However, since I was leaving for New Orleans in a month and needed some of the big money that came with working at O'Farrell's, I decided to take the plunge.

On a Monday night—O'Farrell's auditions were only held on Monday nights—I gathered all my confidence into a little ball and headed to the seedier side of the Tenderloin, Polk and O'Farrell to be exact.

I told the guy at the ticket booth that I was there to audition, and he pointed to a small room on his right that held a couple of couches and chairs, a coffee table strewn with magazines, and about ten wannabe O'Farrell strippers. Since there was no place left to sit, I stood, pretending to read a magazine while we all snuck looks at one another, smiling and turning away whenever we caught someone else's eye.

Eventually, a middle-aged woman entered the room, thanked us all for coming, and told us to stand up, please. After carefully inspecting us for a few minutes like an army drill sergeant, she began pointing with her pen at certain women. "You." "You." "And you." I was the seventh and final dancer selected. The rest were politely dismissed and encouraged to come back the following week. Those of us who remained followed the woman through a maze of stairs and small rooms that eventually led to the "backstage" area, which was nothing more than a dusty room with a few mirrors. We were told to change into our outfits.

Once I was ready, I gave the woman the name of the song I would be dancing to. You were allowed only one song, and if you received a card after you were finished, then you'd been hired. I was fourth in line, between two blondes, which was good because I'd stand out.

I tried to relax while I waited my turn, which proved to be impossible because of the reactions of the other dancers as they came offstage. "Jesus, the lights," was all I heard as they ran past me, blinking madly and grabbing at towels.

Finally I was up. I stepped onto the stage, and, instead of looking away, stared directly into the harsh white lights above. Then I looked down onto the enormous stage, its smooth polished hardwood gleaming. I could feel the audience on both sides staring at me expectantly, but I couldn't see their faces. I took a deep breath, feeling like a gladiator in the arena, the audience a mob of blood-lusting spectators.

I had chosen Cab Calloway's "Minnie the Moocher." As Mr. Calloway began to "hidee-hidee-ho," I strutted down the freshly waxed hardwood, my head at a downward angle as I tried to focus on an audience I couldn't see. The pole at the very end of the stage beckoned in the distance and once I reached it, I held on to it with one hand, feeling the wetness on the brass from the previous dancer. With my free hand, I rolled my long, tight Lycra-nylon cherry-red dress down past my hips to my ass, then farther, down my thighs. I heard a few whistles in the distance as my dress came off completely, dropping limply to the floor. I was nude, my ass, stomach, hips, tits, torso, hair, and lips swaying toward the unseen crowd as I twirled around the pole. More whistles, a few yells, and it was over.

"She's cute, tip her," I heard a woman say as I was walking offstage, and when I took a closer look, I saw it was another dancer, smiling at me. Out the corner of my eye, I saw bills scattered all over the stage.

At the end of the audition, all the dancers had to parade onstage together. Seven of us stood naked before the invisible audience, helpless before our judges. They could see everything: our scars, our anxieties, our need to be wanted as we sacrificed ourselves before something omnipotent and seemingly larger than ourselves—club management—saying with our cutest faces, Please hire me, please choose me. We may as well have been on our knees.

First place went to a dancer named Carmen, a blonde with large (false) breasts, and glittering rhinestone boots. I also got a card and was told that I'd been hired at the O'Farrell Theatre for my unusual taste in music and my exotic looks.

Two days after I received the card, I sat in an office working out my schedule with Percy, a slight, thin-mustached, dark-haired John Waters look-alike. I was to work the day shift at first; Percy told me that you had to "earn" the highly coveted night shifts. This wasn't a problem for me, as I was still spending my evenings at Gigi's.

My main work was to be done in the New York Live room, where I had auditioned. "I don't know if you want to work in the other rooms," Percy offered, and I shook my head. The O'Farrell Theatre was dubbed the "Adult Disneyland" for the various sexual attractions it offered, which provided something for nearly every man's sexual fantasy. However, all I wanted to do was dance, plus do lap dances, which I had learned to endure.

The women at O'Farrell's were exactly how I expected them to be: beautiful and fiercely businesslike. They were on their cell phones constantly, talking to regulars, talking to management about giving them more shifts, talking to real estate agents about the new houses they'd recently purchased. I looked at these cool, calculated women and thought, Corporate strippers. They made the dancers at Glitterati's and Ruby's look like amateurs.

In addition to the New York Live stage, I also worked the Wall

Dance room, where customers got lap dances standing up, hence the name, and the Cine Stage, or Sinner's Stage, a dark room where men watched nonstop porn flicks on a huge screen.

The dancer's job in the Cine Stage room was to go around and give men lap dances to help them obtain release. For me, this became an act of absolute subtlety. I learned to glide silently down the aisle until I got to the man's side, discreetly trying to determine if he'd been recently "relieved" by another dancer. I could tell by his posture: If he was stiff (no pun intended), or if he shifted in his seat, or if his eyes darted around the room (often their eyes were glazed over, so it was hard to tell), then I sweetly asked if he'd "like some company." The entire routine was based on my ability to materialize from out of nowhere, like an unexpected, cool breeze on a hot day. My movements had to be graceful enough to be recognized, yet subtle enough to not intrude on the fantasy, which I was now becoming part of. If he hadn't had his release, he took out the money without hesitation, without giving me a second, sometimes not even a first, look.

There was no set price to these "dances"; it was all about how long we grinded and squirmed on their laps. No man dared to give anything less than a five, and five dollars could mean two minutes, or five seconds, depending on how we felt. If he gave less up front, a dancer would stay until he gave more. If he gave a ten, he definitely wanted the dancer to stay a little longer, so she'd do a couple minutes. However, for me a ten meant one minute, a five maybe twenty seconds. I measured time my own way; there weren't any clocks around, and I wasn't sitting there counting in my head. It was a feeling, an observation of the man's breathing patterns, or the degree of aching in my thigh muscles. Sometimes I would use a nearby dancer as a marker.

There was nothing emotional in this work; this wasn't about intimacy. There was no hair or face touching, no holding hands or gazing into eyes, not a single shared smile. Sometimes not even a word. There was a huge dichotomy between sexual fantasy and intimacy in this room. The man was at the mercy of whatever was projected onscreen.

I'd never worked in such an environment before, and it was quite intimidating. It was made a bit easier by a small bottle of Old Crow, which I sipped on the sly while freshening up in the dressing room.

On my final night in San Francisco, I went out with the core group from Gigi's for one last drink.

"To your new life," they toasted me.

"This was the only club where I've ever felt really comfortable," I confided. And it was true. The dancers at Gigi's were the closest I had to friends, even though they thought my approach to stripping was rather unorthodox.

"You'll be back," Divine assured me with a sadistic smile.

I threw her a look and she just shrugged.

"Are you going to dance down there?" Amber asked.

"I don't think so."

"Yeah, you probably will," Sabrina said. "It's not that easy to get out, you know."

"You don't leave when you're on top of the world," Divine added.

"As far as stripping, your ego is so intact right now,," Haley said, lighting a cigarette. "You're in goddess mode, girl."

"It's hard to quit when it's like that," Katiya sighed, inspecting her empty shot glass. "The money's just too good, you're in control, you're glowing, the world loves you . . ."

"Yeah, but then all of a sudden you crash hard," Divine said seriously. "Out of nowhere it kicks your ass and you start to feel and look like shit." She gave a hard little laugh. "That's what we're all waiting for."

"Jeez, it isn't that bad all the time," Haley argued.

"You've only been dancing for about as long as Layla has," Divine reminded her. "You'll hit bottom one day, sweetheart."

"And the worst thing about it is that you don't really feel the bottom," Savannah said softly. "You just feel really shitty all of a sudden and don't know why."

"But I'd like to quit while I'm ahead," I said.

They just laughed and shook their heads.

eighteen

I stayed in Florida with my family for a few days, enough time for me to read *A Confederacy of Dunces*, which I considered my introduction to New Orleans life. Then it was time to go. As my mother and grandmother waved from the window, I drove off in my new Ford Topaz, which I didn't trust entirely after it stalled several times that afternoon. But I was in too good a mood to really worry about it—I had so much faith in the new direction my life was about to take and was sure this faith would carry me through whatever trouble arose.

It felt invigorating to hit the road. The afternoon was sunny and hot as I cruised along I-95, the humidity radiating through my car windows, which I had left open in order to feel my hair whip around in the wind. I popped in a Frank Sinatra tape and sang along to "Witchcraft" as loudly as I could. "Those fingers in my hair / That sly come hither stare." Life was good.

Then, in a matter of seconds, life wasn't so good. The sky went from sunny to black, followed by rain so hard I couldn't see the road in front of me. It happened so quickly that I didn't even have a chance to roll up the window. Drivers hit their brakes, and I was now crawling along at about ten miles per hour. Within a few seconds, though, the rain was gone and everything was clear again. I accelerated to seventy, the car seat sticking to my wet ass as I sang at the top of my lungs. "Proceed with what you're leadin' me to!"

This was the way it went for the rest of the journey through Florida: sun, Sinatra, then heavy rain, then sun, then more Sinatra, then torrential rain again, and on. I wondered why the hell they called it the Sunshine State. Talk about false advertising. The Psychotic Weather State was more accurate. Or the Never-Ending Everglades State, as I drove through endless stretches of swampland, the scenery like a looped film forever repeating itself.

I finally arrived at the guesthouse in New Orleans, where Rick, beer in hand, greeted me and helped bring in my luggage and boxes. He gave me a private room upstairs; I paid for the first two nights, and we arranged for me to begin work later that week.

"Sleep well," he slurred with a lazy drunken smile, then shut the door on his way out.

I sat on the bed, which thankfully wasn't too squishy this time, and began to write in my journal, then stopped because I didn't know what to say about uprooting my life the way I just had. The world was suddenly a blank canvas, and everything beckoned, the way it had when I'd first moved from Los Angeles to San Francisco. Only now I hadn't moved to break away from home; I had moved to break away. Period.

I spent the next few evenings working for my room and board. My shifts weren't long, only about four hours, and all I did was check people in, give them their keys, and show them to their rooms. Most of the guests were European tourists with enormous backpacks strapped to their bodies, who only wanted a room for a night or two before heading to their next destination, and the destination after that. It seemed a pointless way to travel, to visit a place for a day to say you'd "been there." "Trophy Tourism," a European friend of mine once called it. Most of the time was spent on a Greyhound bus, which didn't seem like much of a vacation.

During the day, I hung out in a coffee shop, writing and scouring the newspaper for places to live. One afternoon, two men sat down at a nearby table and started talking about how they needed a roommate. Without realizing what I was doing, I got up and walked over to them.

"You guys need a roommate?" I asked.

"Yeah, we do," one of them said. "Hi, I'm James, and this is Andrew." He pointed to the dark-haired, green-eyed man across from him. Andrew scanned my face and mumbled a hello. I stared back at him and immediately wanted to touch his face, which was a disturbing feeling because I'd never had the urge to do that to anyone before.

"It's a house in the Irish Channel," James said as I tried to pay attention to his words. "Huge house, cheap rent. Four people will be living there."

"Well, I'm going to need a place to live soon," I offered impulsively, then wondered how it was that my mouth could open so quickly and form words without my brain thinking a single thought.

"Awesome," James said, casting a glance at Andrew. "Unless Jeannine gets her friend to come into town."

"I don't think she's coming," Andrew said, shifting in his seat. He turned and stared at me; I stared back.

"I think Jeannine wants to go back and see the house," James said.

"Who's Jeannine?" I asked, suddenly annoyed.

James cocked a thumb at Andrew. "His girlfriend."

The following week, on my birthday, I met James and Andrew at a place called the Dragon's Den, a restaurant-bar on the edge of the French Quarter. The Dragon's Den was divided into two floors; the downstairs was a Thai restaurant, while upstairs was a strange bar that looked like an opium den, complete with red lights and red cushions to sit on.

The bar was crowded, so we went outside to the balcony and took a small table off to the side. The smell of pot hung in the air, and I spotted three different tables passing around joints in plain sight. James said that this was common in New Orleans.

We were waiting for Jeannine to get off work, since it was only natural for her to meet me if we were all going to be living together. I was not looking forward to meeting her.

James looked around. "She may not find us out here," he said. "I'd better go inside, in case she's looking for us."

"She'll find us," Andrew said glumly.

But James had already gone inside. I got out a cigarette and looked around for some matches. Andrew reached for his Zippo and flicked it a few times. It didn't work. He flicked it a few more times, until it finally offered a low flame. He leaned in close to me, and I leaned in close to him. My hand shook nervously as I held the cigarette to my lips. He lit it and looked at me. I looked at him. When it was finally lit, I leaned back in my chair, but Andrew remained hunched forward, staring at me.

"Why are you looking at me like that?" I finally asked, determined to break the sexual tension.

He laughed loudly as I felt my face flush.

I lay in bed as dawn approached. The lights in the room were still on. It felt like someone had struck a match to my insides and I'd been ignited. Of course I would choose a taken man to be taken with. And it was rare for me to be taken with anyone, especially so quickly and unexpectedly. I didn't know what was happening, but something powerful drew me to Andrew, and it had nothing to do with brains or looks or anything that tangible. All I knew was that a switch flipped inside me when I looked at him, and I couldn't explain how or why, which infuriated me, because there wasn't much in my life I wasn't able to explain or rationalize.

When I finally slipped into sleep, the sky was light with morning and the voices between waking and dreaming were indistinguishable.

nineteen

A week later, I moved into a big house on Constance Street. Since Jeannine and James worked during the day, and Andrew and I didn't (Andrew didn't seem to work at all), the two of us immediately began to spend a lot of time together, often drinking coffee in the afternoon.

Andrew told me about how he had come to New Orleans for inspiration and to work on his painting. I nodded a lot and stared at his face, trying to rationalize my feelings for him. It was inevitable, I reasoned, that with a group of young people sharing a house together, there would be some underlying attraction. Of course, I conveniently ignored the fact that I'd been attracted to him before moving in. I instead told myself that these feelings were fleeting and that we could just be "friends." See, we were being friendly, just having a friendly cup of coffee together, and a friendly conversation. Friendly, friendly, friendly. I obsessively chanted the words to myself.

One day he asked me what I did for work in San Francisco.

"I danced," I said, smiling and looking down at my coffee.

"Really? What kind of dancing?" he pressed.

"Stripping." It sounded like such a come-on.

"Really?" he replied, lighting a cigarette. "Do you still? Dance?"

I shook my head. "No, I don't dance right now, and I don't think I will, but . . ." I hadn't thought about dancing for a while, and now that I was being flat-out asked about it, I wasn't sure how I felt.

"I think it's interesting," he said, interrupting my thoughts. "I think it's sexy."

I laughed.

"No, not like that. I mean, I think it's sexy that you did it," he said. "I don't know about the job being sexy, but I think it's sexy that you did it, because you're different."

Sometimes I tried to break our coffee tradition by leaving the house and wandering around the French Quarter, ostensibly looking for a job. I had enough money to last me a good while, but I needed something to do to stop me from dwelling on my feelings for Andrew.

I walked up and down Bourbon Street, past some upscale strip clubs, which I walked by quickly. I went down Decatur Street, past some tiny strip clubs, freakish and dark. I looked inside, curious, then stopped myself. There's got to be a better way to make money, I told myself firmly. But I longed for the stage; I missed leaning against the pole and writhing on the dance floor. I missed the clarity of my dancing identity, and how easy it was to focus on the moment and my body and nothing else. I needed some clarity, because nothing made much sense.

And so I returned once again to the stage, this time out of a strange desperation.

The Dollhouse was unlike any club I'd ever worked in. While the dancers at Gigi's were gritty yet perky, the dancers at the Dollhouse were haggard and run-down. A couple of them looked to be pushing forty, or fifty, and many seemed to have drug problems. It was rumored that a dancer named Marie, a scrawny woman with long, straight hair, kept her nipples covered with black tape because she was a junkie and shot up through her nipples. I wasn't one to listen to rumors, but one night I walked into the bathroom and saw her with a needle poised at her breast. I quickly shut the door.

Another dancer was five months pregnant. She took to the stage wearing black seven-inch heels and a long black cape, her belly protruding through the black fabric like a luminous full moon on a dark night. She added to the effect by powdering her belly and cradling it in her hands onstage, as though it were the star attraction. A few other women were three to four months pregnant but still hadn't made up their minds whether they wanted to keep the babies. Those who weren't pregnant or junkies were covered in tattoos and chain-smoked like crazy, knocking back shots as they gave deep, guttural laughs to their customers. It was the weirdest, seediest stripping scene I'd ever experienced, and I felt like I was rubbernecking at a gory accident. Usually, such working conditions would have made me run out screaming, but

I didn't, and I couldn't explain why; the air of shadiness somehow kept me paralyzed.

The doorman, Lenny, a man in his fifties, drew me aside one night after I had finished a set. He shook his head at me in disbelief.

"Darlin', what the hell are you doing here?" he asked, a cigarette dangling from the corner of his lips. "A pretty girl like you ought to be in a class joint, not this hell hole."

"I hate upscale clubs," I said. "They don't let me move the way I like."

"Honey, you can't always do what you wanna do," he chided with a chuckle.

"Yes, I can," I replied. I liked how fatherly he was to me.

He squinted at me through a cloud of cigarette smoke. "Well, at least save your money, sugar, so you got something to show for being in this lousy business."

I smiled at him. "It's not so lousy."

He raised his eyebrows. "Stick around here for a while."

Jeannine tried not to glare at me too much when she found out what I did for a living. She was a beautiful woman with clear skin, dark lashes, full lips, and a slender neck that gave her a look of elegance and frailty. Yet there was nothing elegant or frail in her dislike of me. I could feel her animosity when she passed me in the house and didn't acknowledge my existence, or when she ignored me when I spoke. She wasn't outspoken in her hatred, but I could feel it so I tried to avoid her. When I did run into her, she was always cleaning, and if Hole wasn't blasting from the stereo, then it was

Billie Holiday moaning woefully. I interpreted the schizophrenic music taste as a combination of her hatred toward Andrew and me, and self-pity.

Sometimes, we attempted to talk, particularly about things mystical, which interested us both, but having something in common (besides Andrew) didn't help.

One night she tried to do a tarot reading for me, but, understandably, her feelings of resentment got in the way.

"You're using your sexuality in a negative way," she said, gazing down at the cards, then studying her tarot book. "Your femininity is coming out all wrong, Rania—see the Empress card, which represents feminine power, and how it's reversed? You lure men in with your sexuality and body, but it's not the right kind of femininity."

I wanted to hurl the tarot book at her goddamn head, but I calmed myself down before opening my mouth.

"Couldn't the Empress reversed represent a female presence that doesn't trust me or like me?"

She blinked and shook her head. "I don't think so."

"You're sure?"

"Well, it's not like women are going to like you for being that way," she mumbled.

I didn't say anything.

"I think you need some help," she went on. "Find other options, a better way of making money. Maybe get a loan and go to a vocational school or something."

"A vocational school?"

"Yeah, it's a school where you learn working skills. What's so funny?" she asked when I started laughing.

"I know what a vocational school is," I said, still laughing. I knew I was being obnoxious, but I couldn't help it; part of me wanted to slap her.

"I think it's your dancing," she said gently. "Don't you think it effects your sexuality? Have you ever thought of that?"

Of course I had. I wanted to explain to Jeannine what it was like to dance, because I'd really never told anyone; I'd never even written about it in my journal. But it was pointless to try to explain anything to her because I didn't even know where to start, and I was sure she didn't give a shit anyway. Besides, half the time I didn't even understand what was happening inside me.

I didn't have to explain anything to Jeannine because three weeks later, she and Andrew broke up. She was moving back to New York or something. The night before she left, she threw herself a going-away party, a few of her friends showing up with bottles of wine and candles. They locked themselves in her bedroom for hours, and the next morning, she left without a word to anyone in the house.

That same night, Andrew and I ended up at a tiny bar uptown called Snake and Jake's, a seedy but popular little hangout whose only illumination came from strings of Christmas lights. We grabbed a couple drinks and took a corner table. The conversation, the words and sentences we exchanged, whizzed past me entirely.

Later that night, we made out in my car, the tension between us exploding after four months of forced self-control. The dam burst; the saliva flowed, and we devoured each other.

Over the next few weeks, I yielded my body to Andrew in a way I had never yielded it to anyone in my life. It scared me, it terrified me, and it made life worth living. But it didn't last; before long, things had changed between us, from romantic bliss to a bad twentysomething sitcom.

The first problem was that I was the sole breadwinner. This didn't bother me until I started coming home to find Andrew lazily strumming a guitar and talking to James about forming a band. It reminded me of the old stripper joke:

> What does a stripper do with her asshole before work?
> She drops him off at band practice.

Some days James would head to the Quarter to play the saxophone on the street for extra income. Andrew began to accompany him, bringing a bucket and wooden spoon to "jam." Whenever I saw them, I walked the other way.

"You guys shouldn't do that," I told Andrew one night as we lay in bed. "You shouldn't rip people off like that."

"We're not ripping them off!" he said passionately. "We're giving them music, and it's their choice to pay or not."

"But you're not homeless or anything," I argued. "Why act like you are?"

"Are you ashamed of me?"

"I am," I said, which threw him off. He hadn't expected me to be that blunt.

"You think you're better than street performers? Is that it?" he shot back.

I sighed loudly. "No, but even the street performers care enough about what they do to actually get licenses, Andrew. You're just doing this for spare change. You don't even play the drums!"

"I do now."

I didn't say anything.

"You're a snob, Rania," he stated. "Do you know that?"

I ignored the remark. "I don't know why you're not trying to sell your paintings," I said instead.

"No gallery wants them, that's why."

"Did you even try?" I asked.

"No, but I know what they like. They like all that New Orleans tourist stuff. They wouldn't appreciate my work."

"I've passed by a few that weren't like that on Julia Street," I offered. "They had some interesting work."

"They're all shit," he grumbled.

It sounded to me like Andrew was the real snob. When I said this to him, he grew angry and denied it. "You don't get it!" he yelled. "I don't want my paintings hanging in one of those places."

I wanted to tell him that not all the places were like that, but then stopped myself. Why was I trying to convince him to do anything? I wasn't his mother, yet our relationship was beginning to resemble one of parent and child.

Andrew fell into a deep depression. I didn't know what his problem was, and he wouldn't talk to me when I asked. I suspected it was the weed, which he now smoked every day. When he didn't have any, he acted like someone's pissed-off dad, which was annoying behavior for a twenty-five-year-old man. We began to fight more and more, as he started to complain that I was "never home," which was accurate, because I was usually either writing at the coffee shop or dancing.

To top it off, I often came home from work to find impromptu get-togethers that included what seemed like every homeless charlatan in the French Quarter. People with names like Weevil, Treestump, and Eulogy ran amok through the house, eating our food and drinking our wine. The smells of pot, patchouli, and body odor wafted through the halls as I made my way upstairs, desperate for some peace and quiet after an evening at the Dollhouse. One night, however, I entered our room to find a young woman named Hestia sprawled out on my bed, leafing through my journal.

"Do you mind?"

Hestia's faded black lipstick puckered dramatically as she put down my notebook. "Oops. Sorry. Is this yours?"

"Yeah, it's mine," I said. I couldn't decide whether to kill her or laugh at her.

"Well, um . . ." she giggled, sliding off the bed. "It's good. Trippy mind-fuck stuff." Astonished, I watched her walk out the room, wondering if she'd raided my underwear drawer. As Hestia's great leather boots clomped down the stairs, I picked up my journal from the bed and held it close.

Andrew's mood also began to affect our sex life, which had once been so incredible. Now, I would try and get something going, and he would evade my touches, backing away when I tried to be intimate. I had my own suspicion as to why but didn't mention it until one night when he pulled away as I tried to unbutton his shirt while we were sitting on the couch.

"It's the dancing, isn't it?" I asked.

"No," he said. Then he got up from the couch and looked away. "Okay, fine, maybe a little, okay, yeah."

"You never had a problem with it before," I pointed out.

"Yeah. I thought it was sexy before," he mumbled.

I reached for him again. "And now?"

"I think you should quit," he said, pulling away again. "I think it's affecting us."

I laughed. "Oh, is that all that's affecting us, my dancing?"

"Don't you think so?" he asked seriously.

"No, I think it's good to blame my dancing because it's an obvious thing."

He angrily got up and fixed me with a look. "You know, Rania, you justify anything just to argue. Are you even happy dancing?"

"No, I kind of hate it," I said, surprising myself. "But I don't know what else to do."

"Quit," he said desperately. "Just quit already."

"Because I hate it or because you're jealous?"

"Jesus!" he yelled. "Why does it even matter?"

"Because it does," I said. I knew I was being hard on him, but I wanted to quit for myself, not for the sake of the relationship. I just didn't know how to reconcile my need for independence with Andrew's needs, and I feared that I was going to be making a mistake no matter what I did. So, as was my nature, I dug my heels, paralyzed at the thought of losing Andrew, paralyzed at the thought of losing something that had become a part of me, the dancing, even though I no longer wanted it to remain part of me.

"It isn't for you to tell me when I should quit," I said stubbornly.

"Don't you even care that we're falling apart?" he yelled after me as I left the room. "What the hell is wrong with you?"

I didn't know what was wrong with me. I just couldn't stand him caging me in this way.

I packed my clothes for work. He yelled again, "What are you doing?"

"I'm going to work," I said.

"No," he said. "You're staying here with me."

"Right," I said, going downstairs. He followed me.

"Don't go," he said. "You're gone all time."

"I'm not dancing all the time I'm gone!" I exclaimed. "I write during the day!"

"Well, then stay here with me and write."

"No."

"Why not?" he asked.

"Because I don't want to. I'm just not comfortable here."

"Why not?" he pushed, and I blew up.

"Because this isn't about my dancing, it's also about your goddamn pot bullshit and your possessive bullshit. Until you solve your own problems, don't point your finger at me." I was screaming; he started to walk away. I threw down my bag.

"Oh, " I yelled. "Are you walking away now? Have I upset you?

Is this bothering you? So you're the good guy and I'm the goddamn slut! Is that it? Never mind the fact that you want me in your little golden cage."

"Shut up!" he screamed.

"To sing in a goddamn golden cage for you."

"You are so over the top," he said tiredly. "You can't even see yourself."

"I see myself from every fucking angle at work every fucking night!" I screamed. "Do you really think I want to see it at home?" I left and slammed the front door behind me, then almost threw up in the bushes because I was so angry.

twenty

In January, the Dollhouse got taken over by new management. Always wary of new management in strip clubs, I quit the place and began working next door at a club called the Dream Den. Lenny came over with me and became the manager.

The Dream Den was somewhat bigger than the Dollhouse, and the stage was located behind the bar, so that when a customer was seated on his bar stool, the dancer was right above him. The surface of the stage was filthy (despite being scrubbed clean each night), and at the end of a set, my knees, elbows, and the palms of my hands were always blackened with dirt. Since all the strippers knew the condition of the stage, I was one of the few who did floor work.

The Dollhouse had had its share of haggard dancers, but the Dream Den was an honest-to-goodness freak show. Snaggle-toothed young women, cross-eyed dancers with limps, junkies, girls with tattoos on every centimeter of their bodies, drag queens, you name it, they worked there. I stood out as wholesome as a glass of milk by comparison.

One night, I watched as a tall Goth stripper wearing a big black wig shot up in the dressing room. She had her hand positioned over the sink, a needle sticking into one of the veins in the back of her hand. With the other hand, she filled the needle with tap water, then injected it into the throbbing, protruding vein as blood trickled from her hand.

"What are you doing?" I asked, and she told me that she needed to dilute the dope in her bloodstream.

Prostitution abounded in the Dream Den. In dark booths topped with red lights (which, I learned later, were turned on to warn the dancers when the club was being raided), anything went: blowjobs, hand jobs, sex. All this was no dark secret and was openly discussed among the dancers, who brought condoms to work and talked about how lousy a lay a particular customer was.

Drag queens lured in young men, gave them mind-numbing head, then convinced them that they were in love. During my first week, Cecile, a tall, dark drag queen with monstrous breast implants, became engaged to a customer.

"He don't know what he's got himself into," she sighed as she squatted on the toilet, her miniskirt hitched up, her large hands, painted with bright red nail polish, directing her cock into the bowl.

"You mean he doesn't know you're ..." my voice trailed off as she looked at me and started laughing.

"Hell, no, girl, you think I'm crazy?"

"But wait till the honeymoon," Angela, a thin queen with a regal neck, purred. "He'll be down there and your big fat cock's gonna be waiting, all ten inches—"

"Shut the fuck up, bitch." Cecile bit off the words as she snapped off some toilet paper, wiped, then stood straight, pulling up her G-string. "I take care of my man, and that's why he keeps coming back."

The cops came in constantly and sat at the bar drinking beer. I soon learned that they were regular customers, getting action from the dancers on the side. One night in the dressing room, I overheard Leslie, the bartender, telling one dancer, a tall, thin speed-freak with frosted hair, to pack her things because one of the cops, Dave, wanted her to go home with him. Then Leslie turned to me.

"Layla, I know you're probably going to say no," she said. "But Dave's partner, Dan, wants to take you out for breakfast."

I looked at her through the mirror as I slid on some lipstick. "No."

"He's a nice guy," she assured me, but I shook my head. She leaned over to whisper into my ear. "He really likes you."

"No."

"Suit yourself," she sighed.

When I made my way to the club floor, Dan motioned me over.

"Just breakfast?" he pleaded, and I smiled, shaking my head. He was clean-cut and beefy, with the look of an ex-Marine.

"I don't mean no disrespect," he said with a smile. "I just want to talk to you for a while, that's all. Is it a crime for a man to wanna get to know a lady over a little breakfast?"

"You should be the one telling me if it's a crime," I told him. Lenny quickly came over and pulled me to the other side of the bar.

"How are you, darlin'?" he asked me. "That dirty cop bothering you?"

"Dirty? I thought he was just a nice policeman," I replied.

"Why, he's a gentlemen, of course," Lenny said in his thickest Southern accent. He lit a cigarette, inhaled, and blew out a fat stream of smoke.

Garth Brooks played on the jukebox as Cecile, clad in cowgirl gear, a sheriff star pinned to her enormous red bra, shimmied around the stage. The two cops looked away when she jiggled her huge jugs in their direction. I used this as an opportunity to make my getaway.

One evening, a drunken young man stumbled in and wanted me to dance for him. Drunks were the worst customers because their behavior was so unpredictable. Rarely did you encounter the good-natured happy drunk; more often, they were outraged at the world and everyone in it, and whoever got in their way was going to pay, by having to listen to nonsensical blathering about how the world sucked, by being the target of physical aggression, or by being hit with one of the old standbys, puke and/or piss.

Even after I turned him down for a dance, the drunk invited me to sit with him and another dancer named Rosie, an older woman with a ravenous cocaine appetite and a feathered hairdo, who rouged her nipples. I decided to try and make the best of the situation, and at least make some money.

He wanted us both to dance for him, so we pushed him to buy us a large bottle of champagne. This was the ever popular "champagne scam," where a customer bought a bottle for the dancer and took her to a back booth, where she danced for him for as long as the champagne flowed out of that bottle. There were four sizes, ranging in price from thirty dollars to five hundred dollars. The champagne was the worst quality you could imagine; they bought it for ten dollars a case. And it gave you the runs.

The man stated that he didn't like champagne.

"It's not for you, it's for us," I informed him. "If you want something else to drink, then buy yourself something else."

Rosie giggled and cooed into his ear, but he kept ogling me, trying to reach for my thigh. I slapped his hand away every time. However, I managed to talk him into buying us a magnum (five hundred dollars). Rosie gave me a thumbs-up.

"You guys can dance for him upstairs in the storage room," Leslie told us in the dressing room. The smell of cigarettes and shit filled the air. Lenny came in as Leslie left.

"Are you girls ready?" he asked us. I turned to Rosie, who was slipping a few condoms into her purse.

"But ..." I said.

"What's wrong?" she asked.

"Just get upstairs, Rosie," Lenny said sharply. She shrugged, slung her purse over her shoulder, and left the dressing room.

"I don't want to–" I started.

"Don't," he said. "Just dance. And if the bastard tries anything, give him a kick in the balls and run down here."

"But–"

"He won't try anything," Lenny assured me. "The guy's too drunk, Layla, trust me."

Shelves of plastic cups, beverage napkins, straws, cleaning supplies, and soap lined the walls of the storage room. The tattered dark brown carpet smelled of mold, and plaster peeled from the ceiling, revealing brown water stains. A shabby plaid sofa had been thrown into the center of the room, the spotlight from a too bright bulb glaring down upon it, making the environment more appropriate for interrogation than for striptease. For a brief moment I missed the cushy setup of Glitterati's. Then the thought was gone, and I was undressing.

The guy watched with drunken droopy eyelids as we pranced around him and danced to the faraway echo of the music vibrating from downstairs mixed with the occasional hollers of rambunctious college kids roaming the streets outside, looking for a good time. We kept refilling his glass, trying to get him to pass out. But he didn't want any more champagne; he wanted to touch and feel. We got him to cough up another couple hundred dollars after much arguing and coaxing, and then Rosie, in a pale satin purple thong, gave him a grinding lap dance, cooing into his ear as I stood far away, pretending to sip champagne from the bottle. But he wanted more.

"Where's the action?" he asked us with a slur. "Shit, when you girls gonna start getting down to business?" Rosie jumped back on top of his lap, but he pushed her off, eyeing me. "Why you all the way over there? Aren't you gonna come over here?"

"Sure," I said, and went over to him. I began to dance, but he kept trying to stuff his hands into the front of my G-string. Fed up as well as nauseated, I shoved him away.

"That's it, I'm done," I said, walking out of the room.

"What the fuck?" the guy asked, craning his head around. "You aren't done yet!"

"The hell I'm not," I muttered, as Rosie followed me to the top of the stairs, the guy cursing and calling us whores. Like that was going to charm me back into his arms.

"I'll try to shut him up," she said. "I'll be down in a minute."

Twenty minutes went by, and when Rosie returned to the bar her lipstick was smeared, her face red and blotchy and her hair mussed.

"He wants you," she told me in exasperation as she lit a Virginia Slim. "He doesn't want me. He put up a big old stink and told me to come right down here and get you."

Lenny listened while we told him the situation. Then he went upstairs but quickly came back down, shaking his head. The guy was a stubborn drunk, and he wanted what he wanted. Now. Lenny chewed on his thumb with a frown for a while and thought, then told us to follow him to the dressing room. When he opened the door, a stripper with dark curly hair was snorting a fat line of something brown on the counter. She saw Lenny and wiped her nose furiously.

"Jill," he said, all businesslike. "We need you, girl."

The drunken guy was lured downstairs, to one of the poorly lit booths, where he was told I would be waiting for him. Only it wasn't going to be me; it was going to be Jill, who had long, curly dark hair like me and was wearing a black bikini similar to the one I was wearing. Aside from that, she looked nothing like me. But to a very drunk, very horny man sitting in a dark room, Jill and I were the same woman.

Before leaving the dressing room, Jill borrowed a condom from Rosie, teased out her hair, and finished her enormous line. Lenny and I returned to the bar, where he told Leslie to get me a drink and reminded me to make sure I gave Jill twenty-five dollars when she was done.

"Twenty-five dollars?" I asked. "Isn't she getting anything else?"

Lenny blew out a steady stream of smoke from his cigarette, then patted me on the arm. "If she's real lucky, she'll have a good time."

I stared at him.

He smiled sadly. "I told you this was a lousy business, didn't I?"

I was in a haze when I got home. Andrew had been painting and came out to serve me some leftovers. I couldn't talk to him about anything that had happened; he'd have freaked out on me. Instead, I tried to act like I was tired, which was not something I needed to fake. I smiled at him over my plate of food as he asked me about my night.

"You made money?" he inquired.

"Yeah, I made some money."

"Good," he said. We were trying to make peace, and I didn't want to upset things. We tried to have a conversation, but I kept spacing out. I finally came to when he asked if he could borrow money.

"Sure," I said, handing over some bills. I didn't even ask what he wanted the money for. I didn't really care, as long as I was left alone.

Later that night while Andrew slept, I lay in bed, staring out the French doors at the trees outside, which looked wintry and bleak against the gun-metal-gray sky. I pretended I was living in another century, in a place I wasn't familiar with.

twenty-one

A week later, a dancer named Caroline returned to the Dream Den. She wasn't new, as she'd worked at the club off and on. But now she was back, with an added extra: She was seven months pregnant.

Lenny and I sat at the bar and watched her onstage; she didn't do much more than walk around the pole and grow tired, then clumsily sit down on the ground, her huge belly before her as she leaned back and lazily took her heavy breasts out of her dress without even bothering to take it off. With a blank expression, she jiggled them a few times. The jukebox rattled out "Low Rider." A few men with drawn faces stared down into their beers and threw bills at the stage. She looked at them with weepy blue eyes and a turned-down mouth. One man finally got up and left. Lenny looked around, shaking his head in dismay.

"Jesus," he mumbled, taking a gulp of his soda. "This is goddamn depressing."

"What are you going to do with her?" I asked, and he shrugged.

"She hasn't got any family, nothing. The boyfriend's gone off someplace, and she doesn't have anywhere to go." He sighed. "I'm letting her stay upstairs in storage until she figures something out."

Caroline climbed off the stage and, hand against her back, headed to the dressing room. The back of her dress was covered with streaks of dirt from the stage. I was next up. Leslie threw me a washcloth and a bottle of rubbing alcohol, which I always used to try to sterilize the stage before I went on. Heading up the little steps that led to the stage, I almost slipped on tiny splattered droplets of liquid. Breast milk.

When my set was done, I went to the dressing room, where I found Caroline on the countertop on all fours, her ass in the air.

"What are you doing?" I asked. She mumbled that she was trying to pass gas without going into labor. "Aren't you only seven months along?"

She shrugged and sniffed. "I think so, but I haven't been to a doctor so I don't know."

"Why haven't you been to a doctor?" I asked. She said that she hadn't had the time and wasn't sure she wanted to keep it, but now it was too late. She wore a tattered white dress with a torn black G-string underneath, and as she made her way down from the counter, she let out an evil fart that nearly sent me staggering against the wall.

"Sorry," she mumbled.

Three weeks later, I entered the dressing room to find Lenny with a bundle of white blankets in his arms and a newborn baby's face peering out curiously, very pink, very disoriented. It suckled on

Lenny's fingers. It was Caroline's baby, born a month premature.

"Just what we need," Cecile grumbled, powdering her nose. "Another crack baby." She snapped her powder compact shut and left the room.

Nobody really knew what was happening with Caroline. She had given birth a couple weeks earlier and had last been seen four days ago at Leslie's place. She had told Leslie to watch the baby while she went out to "run an errand." She was supposed to pick it up a few hours later, but a few hours became a few days, and then Caroline, crying, called Lenny from her friend's house in Alabama, saying she didn't know how to take care of a kid and didn't want to do it.

"So, what now?" I asked.

"Well, Leslie said she'd watch the baby for a while, but he needs a home, so I told Caroline to give it to me. My wife and me are adopting him for now." He looked down at the baby and held it closely. "We never had children. My wife can't. But this is good for us, I think. She's happy; I'm happy. Someone needs to take care of this poor kid." Lenny had a heart in a business that didn't afford you one. He had softness for anyone in pain or in trouble, which didn't work in his favor, as most people took advantage of him.

"Wanna hold him?" he asked eagerly.

I carefully took the baby from him, and looked down at its face; it was puffy, the eyes large and glazed. "Why are his lips so purple?"

"He's a crack baby," Lenny explained. "They get hungry a lot more than normal babies and have to be kept really warm. Caroline didn't even know how to hold him. She slung him over her shoulder like a sack of potatoes when she was walking around."

"Does he have a name?" I asked, pulling the blanket farther over his head.

"Dragon," Lenny said, his lips stretching tightly in disgust.

"Dragon? Are you kidding me?"

"That's what she wants his name to be."

"Are you changing his name?" I asked Lenny, and he shrugged.

"Baby Dragon," I said, and it sounded as weird as I expected it would. I looked down at him as he sucked on my fingers, the soft wet pressure of gums and tongue tingling against my skin. He looked right at my face and blinked; my heart dropped, and my eyes watered and spilled tears on Baby Dragon. I gave him back to Lenny and decided I didn't want to work that night.

"You're back early," Andrew said when I got home. "Not working?"

"No, too many girls," I lied. I made some food and picked at it, unable to eat.

"Why don't you eat?" he asked.

"I'm sorry," I said. "I'm just not very hungry." I lit a cigarette.

"How about some wine?" Andrew asked.

We drank quietly and attempted to play a game of chess in the study. Andrew kept looking at me, but I couldn't look back long enough to hold his gaze. I couldn't concentrate on my game, either. I sat there sipping my wine, spacing out as his bishop grabbed hold of my knight.

"Check," Andrew said, smiling.

"Shit, my queen's gone."

"Are you okay?" he asked.

"I'm fine," I said, rising from my chair. "I'm going to take a shower."

I stood under the hot water forever with my eyes closed, images of the many nights playing out over and over again in my mind: A high-heeled shoe sticking out of a bag, the toilet in the dressing room, the mirror covered with streaks of eyeliner and lipstick, Caroline's belly, the weight of Baby Dragon in my arms, the suckling sensation on my fingers, the cops, the red bulbs in the private booths, a fat line of something to snort, Jill bending down over it. I couldn't tell Andrew about any of this. Knowing that I danced caused enough of a strain for him without my dragging in the nightly dramas. Besides, it was easier for me to keep these things unsaid, because it helped to have my life divided and separate. I kept it all locked away within some dark, forbidden chamber, and when I came home, I wanted simply to let go of all I'd seen and experienced. One day I knew I would have to face all the things I had locked up inside myself, and when that day came, the shit would hit the fan. But that day wasn't here yet, and I was honestly in no rush to welcome it.

We lay together in bed. A short candle blazed on the bookshelf.

"How are you?" Andrew asked, rubbing my shoulder.

"Fine," I said shortly, not wanting to talk.

"Just fine?" he asked, snuggling up next to me. I was in no mood for sex, but I didn't want to reject him and give him another reason not to trust me. As soon as the candle burned out, I climbed on top of him. We moved quietly in the darkness as he watched me from below. I looked away, unable to connect. Our sex life had changed. The intimacy was now forced, a routine to approximate closeness, a method either to drown out the memories of what I'd seen or to reawaken the memory of me. But I didn't really know who I was anymore; I was somewhere between Rania and Layla, more Layla, because I knew who she was. I had made her, crafted her; she was the stuff of my dreams: sexy, smart, and strong. She didn't take any shit, didn't have any inappropriate emotions. She said what she wanted, whenever she wanted to say it. And she had a heart but didn't let it get in the way of being on the stage. She really didn't let it get in the way of anything. She was everything I ever wanted to be: self-made, complete.

I rolled off Andrew and let him hold me, but my eyes stayed wide open, staring out the French doors at the cold, waning moon in the plum-colored sky. If I could've described myself as anything, it would've been that moon, my body and mind as distant and cold as that luminous orb that seemed deceptively closer in New Orleans than it really was.

twenty-two

Four days later, I flew out to visit my family, my heart a clenched fist, hardened against my mother's sudden hysterical concern for my life. I couldn't even look them in their faces, couldn't tell them what was happening to me. Even I didn't know what was happening to me.

Andrew picked me up from the airport when I returned home, and he had some news: James had skipped town. All he left was a note saying he was sorry, but that he was moving to Alaska to weave baskets.

"Weave baskets?"

"That's what he wrote," Andrew said with a shrug, flicking his cigarette ash out the window.

"I don't believe this! What the hell are we supposed to do now?"

"Well, I just got a job at a coffee shop in the Warehouse District," he offered. "But it's only twice a week for lunch."

I felt the cold glass on my window. I turned up the heater and snuggled into my seat.

"At least we have some extra income," I muttered.

The weather grew cold as it got closer to Mardi Gras, the winter chill, combined with New Orleans's ever-present humidity, soaking through my clothes and settling into my bones. As a result, I developed a nasty cough that wouldn't go away.

Then the great hordes of Mardi Gras overran the city, drinking, screaming, puking, pissing on lawns, cars, sidewalks, even their own pants when drunk enough, while stoic-looking men stood stationed at street corners, handing out flyers to passers-by about sin and Satan and how we would all burn in hell if we partook of these drunken orgies. I thought we were all in hell already?

Andrew's two shifts a week didn't pay for much, and at the rate we were going, they weren't going to pay for anything, especially when he bought a $250 pair of shoes with his first paycheck. I didn't say anything because I didn't want to nag, but I was furious with his impulsive spending. If it wasn't drugs, then it was shoes. He may as well have been a goddamn stripper!

I gave six hundred dollars to George, the landlord, which was two hundred short of the rent. He asked when the rest would arrive, and I told him very soon, in the next week or so. In addition, the gas and electricity, which were in George's name, were also due, and he paid for them up front as he waited for our money. Where was all the money I had made dancing? I had no idea; it just disappeared.

Then my car broke down, and I had to borrow money from my parents to pay for it. My mother screamed at me while I held the phone away from my ear.

As a result of our money troubles, I was forced to get a second job, waiting tables at a bar in the Quarter. The money wasn't as good as I'd hoped it would be, though. Half the time people walked out after ordering drinks, too drunk to realize where they were, or else tried to pay with Mardi Gras beads.

"This isn't the dark ages," I said with irritation when they handed me the beads. "We pay with money here."

But it was the dark ages when George cut off the gas and electricity, since I had never given him the two hundred dollars we owed him, then told us we had until the beginning of March to get the hell out. We were officially squatters now. We had to wear sweats and socks to bed and cover ourselves with three or four blankets to avoid freezing to death. We also had to use candles for light, until Andrew discovered that the electricity in the storage room was still on and he ran an extension cord from there to our room. He also found a tiny TV set and brought it into our bedroom, where we lay together each night, watching Letterman as we ate takeout.

"You're a genius," I said, giving him a kiss on the cheek.

My cough worsened with the cold and the fact that I was working double shifts every day, coming home at about three-thirty each morning from the Dream Den to get four hours of broken sleep, interrupted by my coughing and hacking, before getting up at nine in the morning to work at the bar. One day my cough got so bad that I had to go to the emergency room, where I was diagnosed with walking pneumonia and bronchitis.

"Stop smoking," the doctor advised.

"That's it?" I asked.

"Get some sleep too," he said. He prescribed some antibiotics, but I kept working the same backbreaking shifts, hoarding as much money as I could while I scoured flyers and responded to ads, looking for a new place for us to live. I was doing all the looking, making all the calls, setting up the appointments, even though Andrew was still only working his two lunches a week. He never volunteered to help, and whenever I asked, he shrugged and nodded. I also started to notice that money was missing from my purse, twenty dollars here and there. I was sure it was Andrew, yet I didn't want to bring it up, in case I was wrong. Still, I began checking ads for places to live alone.

Mardi Gras finally ended, which meant that my day shifts were done. I now had time to resume my writing. Each morning, I rose from the covers, teeth chattering, as Andrew sat up in bed groggily.

"Where are you going?"

"To write, where else would I be going?"

"You don't want to write here?" he asked.

I sighed. We'd been over this so many times, yet it still wasn't clear to him for some reason.

"We've got coffee here," he said. "I'll make you some, a whole pot, just come back to bed." He reached out his arm, looking like a drowning person amid the ridiculous layers of blankets and comforters.

But I didn't want to come back to bed. I was brushing my teeth, washing my face, slipping on my jeans and a sweater, zipping up my ancient black boots. I went to give him a kiss goodbye, and he stared at me glumly.

"Why do you even have to write?" he asked. "Writing's totally overrated. It makes people think too much."

I took a deep breath, then grabbed my backpack. "It makes me happy," I said.

"Words separate people," he argued, lighting a cigarette. "If there were less words, people would be happier."

"Then shut up," I snapped.

"Whatever," he said, lying back down as plumes of smoke rose from his lips. "See you later."

"Yeah," I said, disgusted with the exchange. "Whatever." I slammed the front door on my way out.

Later that night, the drama escalated when I returned from work and found Andrew high on several hits of acid. The moment I walked through the door, he clung to me, eyes bulging. He said he'd been out earlier that night and was scared of his feelings; he said he was attracted to other women.

"Am I supposed to feel bad for you?" I asked, pouring myself a glass of water in the kitchen. I was attracted to other men on occasion as well, but the feelings passed, and I didn't dwell on it. Yet Andrew was terrified of these feelings because he didn't trust himself, and I had a tendency to be jealous, which didn't help the situation.

"Did you make out with someone?" I suddenly asked, feeling my heart sink.

"No, no, I don't love anyone but you," he assured me desperately.

"Are you saying that so you can believe it or because it's the truth?"

"Of course it's the truth!" he exclaimed. "I don't love anyone but you, you're all I have. You make me feel things, Rania."

"Feel things? What does that mean?"

"I don't know, you just bring things up in me, not all good feelings, but I like the fire we have," he said, holding my hand.

I drank my water quietly and tried to absorb his words. I wasn't sure what he was talking about. We were speaking different languages.

"It's too much responsibility," I said. "I don't want to have a specific role like that, to make you feel things. It's too much."

"But it's who you are, it's how you are to me," he told me.

"What about me?" I asked, exasperated. "I want to feel things too; I have a right to that but I have nothing left for myself since I'm just giving it away all the time."

"What are you talking about? Why don't you give to yourself?"

"I don't know, I just can't, I don't know how to," I answered. Then I looked at him. "I give to myself when I write, but you don't support that."

"I do support it, I never said I didn't."

"Andrew," I laughed. "You said writing was a waste of time. But it's something for me. You don't have to love it, but it's a part of me and you have to accept it. I respect what you do, your art. I don't tell you it's a waste of time, so why do you say that stuff to me?"

He looked away.

"There's more to me than being locked up in a room and making you feel things," I went on. "Though I'm not sure you'd be happy to know about it."

"What do you mean?"

I put down my glass and told him that I was thinking of getting a place without him. "Just for a while. We need to try to do things differently because we're stagnating."

"Is it because you want to see other people?" he asked, and I assured him that it was not.

"But I love you," he said, and I told him I loved him too. But I needed to try to quit dancing, and I couldn't afford to carry him.

"If it's the money, then I'll pay you back," he said.

"I don't care about being paid back," I said, and I meant it. "But you don't want to work, and I'm broke. If I had the money, I'd support you, but I'd be dancing to support you, and you don't like my dancing. I need a change, I need a clean slate."

"And you'll wipe me out for it?" he yelled.

"I love you, but you don't trust me, Andrew," I said. "And I've never given you a single reason to think I may want someone else."

"I left Jeannine for you ..."

"If Jeannine means so goddamn much to you then go to New York and get her back!" I screamed.

"No. I want you," he said, pulling me toward him, his eyes bigger than ever. I tried to pull away, but his hand locked tight on my arm. It hurt.

"Let go," I said, but he squeezed my arm even more tightly. I pulled my free arm back and slapped him hard across the face.

"You slapped me!" he exclaimed.

I told him it was over.

"It isn't over," he said. "I love you."

I threw my water glass at him. He ducked, and it shattered when it hit the wall.

"All right, fine," he said, putting up his hands. He left, slamming the front door so hard behind him that it shook the entire house.

I squatted in the middle of the living room and cried for an hour, then passed out in bed.

twenty-three

The following month, I was living uptown in a nice two-story shotgun-style apartment. The area was cleaner, quieter, and much safer than where I had lived with Andrew. My new roommate, Lena, was a Libyan woman who worked in the psychiatric ward at some run-down hospital. Her thick Arabic accent rippled through the house, reminding me of my mother, and when she called my name from the downstairs kitchen, my shoulders always tightened.

"Rrrrrrrron-ya!"

However, she was the ideal roommate because she was hardly ever home. All hours of the day and night, she was gone, tending to her patients.

I quit the Dream Den when Lenny took a temporary leave to take care of Baby Dragon, and I switched to a place across the street called Club Plush. It was large and spacious, and most definitely not upscale, but not as seedy and freakish as the Dream Den. Though the women still had that same run-down look to them, they were prettier, younger, and in better shape.

The simple reality that prostitution was part of the stripping world in New Orleans had been of no great consequence to me, since I refused to sell myself that way. However, the manager at Club Plush, an Irish guy in his forties, didn't care much for my prissy ways, though he didn't say anything directly to me at first.

Things reached a head one Friday night, however, when a customer got pissed off because I wouldn't do more than a lap dance for him. The manager summoned me to a corner of the bar and, sucking on a Budweiser, urged me to go for a "limo ride."

A limo ride was a way for the clubs to avoid getting busted for prostitution. The customer picked his dream dancer and paid five hundred dollars for an hour-long ride through the Quarter in a limousine. It was clear to me what went on inside that limo, yet I feigned ignorance.

"A limo ride?" I asked, raising the pitch of my voice to dingbat level. "What do I do when we're in there?"

"Well, you entertain," he said with a quick shrug.

"So I dance?" I replied, pressing him. "Dance in a car?"

He lit a cigarette, his face growing red with anger. "Well, yeah, real sexy-like dancing and stuff, you know? It's a lot of money for a man to throw down, you don't wanna disappoint him, right?"

"Oh," I looked at him and waited.

"So, you'll do it?" he asked with great annoyance. "You know, it's not easy to get one of these limo rides. I made you a good sale." Then he paused for a moment and threw me a look. "You a cop?" he suddenly asked.

"No," I said, laughing. "Why?"

He sniffed the air and cocked his bushy eyebrow. "Listen, I don't want you working here anymore, you hear me? You got an attitude."

"Fine," I said, then stormed back to the dressing room to gather my things. On my way out, a dancer wearing a tight dress with the Budweiser logo printed on it patted her slightly protruding belly, telling another dancer that she had had an abortion that afternoon. She had been five months pregnant and was now taking a pill to shrink her uterus.

"Can I have one?" the other dancer asked with a giggle.

I decided to try making my rent without taking my clothes off, and I started working the lunch shift at a steak house in the Central Business District. There was a Zen temple located directly above the restaurant (the Zen master owned the entire building), and on occasion, the master would glide downstairs noiselessly in his airy white garments, past the bustling dining area where men and women in business suits were hunched over, devouring thick slabs of steak on their lunch breaks, to complain to the restaurant owner that the fume of smoking meat offended the vegans and vegetarians who were deep in meditation upstairs. The owner, who I learned had flunked the bar exam twice and was now trying his hand at restaurants, just blinked and stared. The real mystery to me was why the Zen master chose to lease the ground floor of his building to a steak house.

As summer in New Orleans began, the heat came on with the sudden intensity of a strange, large aunt I'd never met before locking me into a big bear hug. The air became harder to breathe, and the humidity sunk deeply through my skin, leaving me drenched the second I stepped out the front door.

Still, I ventured out and explored more of the city, at least more of its bars. And I found that, while you could take the girl out of the strip club, you couldn't take the strip club out of the girl. But this time it wasn't a strip club; it was a raunchy little hole off Annunciation Street called Monaco Bob's that featured go-go dancing on Monday nights.

Dubbed "Mammary Mondays," the spectacle consisted mainly of Goth girls, clad in black leather and tattooed from head to toe, dancing on a rickety stage, sometimes adding little touches, like dripping hot candle wax over their flesh. A brass pole rested directly in the center of a tiny stage, and a small runway, consisting of a few nailed-together wooden crates, led to a large iron cage, where the dancers often hung upside down like bats.

Nobody objected the first time I entered the cage and rattled it like crazy, rocking it back and forth on its shaky stand. The Goth girls watched in amusement as I arched my head back, my hair dangling to my ass. Because the environment was grungy and tattooed, I was free to do whatever I wanted. To top it off, there weren't any lap dances; this was strictly go-go dancing, topless style. The manager of Monaco Bob's, a coke-sniffing, redheaded hipster named Joe, paid each dancer twenty-five dollars per night, plus free drinks. In addition, the tips were really good.

For the first time, I could honestly say that people came in for the dancing (and the heavy-handed Goth ambiance), not for companionship or to get off. My relationship to the audience was both mutual and authentic, not to mention lucrative. It had always been my goal as a stripper just to dance. I was sick of the cool hands and cold ways of the "business," sick of quotas and stage fees and rules (and junkies and pregnant strippers). At Monaco Bob's, I was finally free to be what I wanted, to dance the way I wanted to dance, to be appreciated as a dancer and nothing but a dancer.

At the same time I began dancing at Monaco Bob's, I started dating a guy from the coffee shop where I went to write. His name was Ben. Wholesome, fresh-scrubbed, a Loyola student two years younger than me, he'd been slinging coffee there from day one of my involvement with Andrew. Yet I had never noticed him, until one afternoon when he had me howling in laughter as he did a dead-on imitation of some of the college students who came into the coffee shop. He followed this with a goofy impression of Andrew, copying his slow, serious walk, right down to the slumped shoulders and cigarette hanging from the corner of his mouth. He mimicked Andrew's deep voice but did it a few octaves lower, giving it a ridiculous bassy tone. As I laughed, I looked over my shoulder, making sure Andrew wasn't anywhere in sight.

Ben started to call me up at night during his shifts, telling me to look outside at the moon. His voice trembled, as though shocked by the mere presence of it in our solar system. His childlike quality was a refreshing change from Andrew's brooding. Andrew had noticed nothing. Ben noticed everything. People fascinated him, and he loved to copy and mimic, trying on their walks and voices simply to see what it was like to be another person.

His face was round and innocent, with large dark eyes that always looked surprised. He was fastidious with his clothing, a shoe fanatic (the only thing he had in common with Andrew), and a snappy dresser, with shirts always crisp and freshly ironed, his jeans baggy enough to give an appearance of not caring, though he cared a great deal. His hair was cut in a shaggy style, and he fussed with it a lot. He often kept me waiting as he restyled and mussed it until it was just so.

Intimacy with him was soft and comfortable. His sense of humor and his relaxed way made it easier for me to breathe. Raised in a complete, unbroken family, one sister two years younger, a mother and father still in love, he was the antithesis of what I was used to. He regarded me with both fear and fascination.

Lena and I shared a pool with the neighboring house, and one night I coaxed Ben into a midnight swim, stripping off all my clothing and wading into the cool water as I watched him watch me. He got in and splashed around the edge carefully, pretending not to stare. I swam up to him and wrapped my legs around his waist, guiding him inside me. Beneath the glowing full moon he looked at me with widening eyes, a stunned expression on his face. Ben always looked stunned when we had sex, his eyes reflecting a mixture of disbelief and amazement. He turned me this way and that, then compared me to other women when we were done, saying how graceful I was, how sexual I was, fantasy material, really. He told me I was the girl he could never have.

Sometimes he came in to Monaco Bob's to see me dance. "Wow," he would say openly, with no shame. For once, a man I liked was proud of my dancing. As a result, I showed off for him, locking eyes from the stage as his nearly popped out of his head. When I was done, he applauded wildly, looking around to make sure the other men in the audience appreciated me as well. After all the shame Andrew's disdain of my dancing had caused me, I soaked up the attention from Ben like a parched plant does water.

At the same time, Ben was an innocent, which gnawed at me. He had been sheltered most of his life, never wanting for anything, even the most basic thing, like love. Human suffering puzzled him, as he had not been shoved out into the harshness of the world. He would tell me about sad women and men he saw in the coffee shop, friends of his that were distraught; he was a natural giver of sympathy and compassion. Yet at the same time, he would laugh at them, copying their sad voices, even shaking his shoulders to imitate their crying. We both laughed about this: me, unable to cry in front of another person, and Ben, simply innocent of suffering and unknowing of the immense pain heartache could bring.

He gently began to pressure me into exclusivity. However, he'd never had a serious girlfriend before, which made me take a step back. This, of course, made him pursue me even more. Once I told him I liked rosemary, and the next day I found a bunch of it taped to my front door. He left random notes and invitations on my car windshield, and little blue flowers on my doorstep. I smiled to myself, happy with the attention, yet wary as well, because I thought Ben was too concerned with having: everything from clothes to money to education to a certain type of woman. His obvious admiration of me fed my ego, keeping me dangerously elevated, feeling simultaneously coveted yet out of reach—a possession, not a person.

Sometimes on my way to or from work at the steak house, I would see Andrew ambling around town aimlessly, the slumped shoulders, the slow stride, hands shoved in pants pockets, a cigarette dangling from the corner of his lips. I would slow down and offer him a lift to wherever he was going. He would say nothing when he got into the car, as if it was the most natural thing in the world, as if he had been expecting me to come along. I wanted to ask him what he was doing but at the same time didn't really want to know, so I wouldn't say anything, and we usually drove together in silence.

Over the course of several weeks, however, I began to notice that he was rapidly losing weight. He had always been a medium-size man, neither too heavy nor too thin, but now he seemed to be disappearing in his clothes.

One day, I slowed down the car as always, and he got in. Silence.

"Where to?" I finally asked, nearly three blocks later. He shrugged and wouldn't look at me. Silence. So I drove him to my place, where I cooked him a steak I'd snagged from work. As he ate ravenously, I asked him about his situation.

Was he working?

No.

Where was he living these days?

Nowhere really.

Nowhere?

No.

Why didn't he get a job?

He was working on that.

When was the last time he'd slept?

He didn't answer at first. Then he told me that he'd been high for the past few weeks. I flinched, recalling the homeless kids that I had hung out with back in Hollywood and how they'd told me that speed kept them moving and awake and made them forget the hunger. Awake was good when you couldn't find a place to sleep. Awake was good so no one could cut your throat as you slept.

I let him take a shower, then told him to take a nap if he liked. I offered these things nonchalantly, making sure not to make a great show of helping him, so that I didn't injure his pride. He had a hard time sleeping and then asked if he could move in with me. I felt sorry for him, but our relationship was over. I gave him eighty dollars and sent him on his way.

I watched as he walked down the street, shoulders hunched, feet dragging, cigarette smoke trailing behind him. Then he turned around and waved, and when I waved back, he began laughing hysterically, his voice rippling through the street.

twenty-four

A new dancer named Marie joined the go-go freak show at Monaco Bob's. A tall redhead with a loud mouth, she blew into the dressing room late one Monday night, stripped off all her clothes, and began complaining about not having any drugs. Her breasts were plump and freckled, the nipples a deep red.

"Shit," she said, turning to Millie, a statuesque Goth girl with the stance of a high priestess. "I ain't got no fucking speed, you got any?" Millie, lining her eyes, shook her head.

"Shit, honey," she turned to Sadie, a voluptuous blonde. "I'll lick your pussy for some drugs."

"Don't have any tonight," Sadie mumbled, pulling up her black platform boots.

She turned to me. "I'll lick your pussy for nothing," she grinned, sweeping her rather pointed tongue over her teeth. I give her a small smile and returned to my preening.

But onstage Marie was transformed. Her lithe body wrapped around the pole, knowing the rhythm instinctively. I watched her, transfixed, thinking about how our gracelessness was redeemed on the stage, and how the audience was a vital part of that redemption. Most women who strip are emotionally screwed up on some level, and they come to the stage not to forget their shortcomings but to remember their own beauty. For a few minutes, they are transformed, and if they are very good at what they do, others—the audience—will always remember them, and thus they are in a small way immortalized.

One night Andrew came in. He avoided looking at me and instead made a beeline for Marie. I tried not to stare as they talked in a corner, hunched over, giggling. He eventually left, and when it was my turn to dance again, I writhed up against the iron cage only to find Marie slithering up to me. Her glassy eyes vibrated and shook as she lolled out her pointy tongue and made like she was going to lick one of my nipples. She smelled like gasoline and sweat, and I detected the last fuck with Andrew wafting up from between her legs. As she leaned over, my hand came up by itself, involuntarily, and slapped her hard across the face.

She looked at me, stunned, holding her struck mouth. I was stunned too, but went on, not missing a beat. A few men watched with raised interest, hoping a catfight would break out. She finally walked off, speechless, and was nowhere to be found when I left the stage. My tips were extraordinarily good that night.

One day, without warning, the steak house shut down; something about taxes not being paid. So I had no choice but to start stripping again, this time in a dive off Bourbon Street called the Lookie-Bar.

Rania Zada

It was a step up from the Dream Den, but not a very big step.

The manager of the place was a hefty Russian transvestite named Natasha. The cast of characters included Vienna, a heavy-set blonde who always wore thick black boots on the stage and a pin on her bra with a smiley face that read HELLO, MY NAME IS SATAN; Delia, a Goth girl who wore full geisha makeup; Queenie, a big black woman with a mouth full of gold teeth; and my favorite, Vampirella, a psychotic stripper with dyed red hair and a nervous tic. The only way to exchange dialogue with Vampirella was through mirrors; if you spoke to her directly, she wouldn't respond to you.

One of the most fascinating aspects of stripping was the dressing room dialogue, which centered on men when it wasn't about children, since there were so many single mothers in the stripping world. Simply put, there didn't seem to be a single stripper in either San Francisco or New Orleans who had a happy relationship. Boyfriends with drug problems, boyfriends without jobs (I knew that one), boyfriends that cheated, boyfriends suffering from depression or catatonia or evil mood swings or drinking problems or broken motorcycles. There was much of this kind of conversation at the Lookie-Bar. I, however, kept the details of my personal life neatly tucked away, and when they asked me if I had a boyfriend, I nodded, and when they asked what was wrong with him, I said nothing was wrong; he was perfect, wholesome, sweet, cute, caring. They stared at me, and Queenie mumbled that, "maybe you're living in a dream world," and I shrugged, because she was probably right.

As the summer wore on, I wilted, feeling caged in the city. I was dragged down by the heat, the poverty, the stink of it all. New

Orleans was such an intense city—in better moods I loved it, in worse moods I hated it and wanted the hell out. I even considered returning to Los Angeles to go to school but couldn't seem to shake off the rest of my life to actually do it. It was the same old scene: I couldn't find my way into myself or out of myself.

I also became overwhelmed with the need to break things. I began to rummage through recycling bins to find glass bottles, then I'd drive to empty parking lots late at night to smash them against the cement. I went through as many as twenty a night, depending on how fiercely my inner demons screamed. When there weren't enough bottles in the recycling bins, I bought bottles of the cheapest beer I could find. Full bottles were better to break because they sounded like explosions if you slammed them just right.

I also began to have problems working a complete shift at the Lookie-Bar, faking headaches, menstrual cramps, and other ailments so I could get sent home early.

Ben freaked out when he found out that I did lap dances, but he freaked out in his own quiet way, his face turning sad, never angry, his eyes watering with a slight Bambi effect. He asked me about the dances I did, and I told him. I wasn't going to lie. When he asked me if I got turned on, I just looked at him.

"Why would I get turned on?"

He frowned. "Because I would, if I were to get one."

I laughed. "You're a man, of course you would," I told him. "It's my job to make sure you're physically turned on. It's what I'm trained to do, it's my job, nothing else."

But he didn't believe me. He didn't see how I wouldn't be turned on. I thought he was being rather naïve, though I didn't tell him that. However, when he told me he didn't want me to do lap dances anymore, and that it made him uncomfortable, I was no longer tolerant.

"What if I were to tell you to stop working at the coffee shop?" I asked.

"That's not the same."

"Yes, it's the same thing. It's your income, and I'd be asking you to stop making an income."

He looked into his lap; I stood with my hands on my hips.

"Couldn't you do anything else?" he asked me. "Couldn't you take another job? You're bright and capable."

"I know I'm bright and capable," I snapped. "But you want me to change my entire life so that your ego isn't affected by my grinding on some fat middle-aged guy's lap. It's not so much your concern about me as it is your concern of how much of a schmuck it makes you look like." Though I understood why my dancing bothered him, he knew what he was getting into when he started dating a stripper. It was the old argument I had had with Andrew, and now I was having it with Ben.

Out of guilt, I promised to dance for Ben privately, and he responded well to the suggestion. One evening, I materialized on his doorstep clad in a long, black vintage fur coat, with not much else on underneath. He smiled wickedly as I went into the living room, put some music on the stereo, and dragged a chair to the center of the room, then turned off the lights and lit some candles.

I led him to the chair, pushed him down, and got on my hands and knees, working my way up to his lap. His head tilted back as I leaned in to kiss him, sliding my hands over his chest, then down beneath his legs. Suddenly, he nudged me away.

"Is that what you do with your customers?" he asked.

I stood up and said nothing. Did he really think I made out with my customers? Was this a trust issue? Was I not trustworthy because I stripped? I slipped on my coat, cut off the stereo, and switched on the lights. Time passed as I sat on the couch, smoking a cigarette, while he sat in the chair with his hands folded primly on his lap.

"I was doing this for you," I said, breaking the silence. "I thought you wanted it."

"I thought I did."

"Why is a sexual fantasy not enjoyable when it's with me?" I asked him. "If you love me and I love you and want to make a fantasy come true, why is it a problem?"

Why were men so intimidated when asked to integrate intimacy with personal fantasy? Though the fantasy often entailed a body they could describe in detail, right down to the color of each pubic hair, when the face attached to it belonged to the woman they cared for, they couldn't handle it.

"I don't know," he said, looking down at his folded hands. "Maybe because I don't want to share you with anyone else."

But he didn't share me, I thought. Others might experience my physical body, but it was the furthest thing from intimacy. On a deeper level, the problem was that dancing forced me to separate intimacy from physicality and made me turn off my own feelings in order to turn them on in others.

Later that night, I bought two six-packs of beer, drove to a parking lot, and slammed each one against the ground. The explosions fed my fury instead of providing any relief.

twenty-five

I was spending more and more time at work sitting at the bar and sucking down drinks, and less and less time asking men for dances. When I did dance, it felt as though desperation rippled through my skin and dripped out onto the stage.

Vampirella sat next to me, her face looking into the mirror behind the bar.

"You look sad," she said to the mirror.

"I'm not sad," I said, talking back to her vacant reflection. She got up and walked away. I looked back into the mirror, the scenes from the club shining back at me. Delia's geisha face floated through the room as she danced to three minutes of synchronized belching from the jukebox. Customers stared, then tipped her because they didn't know what else to do. Queenie waited to go on next, cleaning her gold teeth with a business card. Natasha filed her manicured talons while screaming at a customer, her thick, intrusive voice booming over the music.

Egyptian Exotica

I looked deeper into the mirror and saw myself as a ten-year-old girl in my family's summer villa in Egypt, crying in front of the luscious Giza sunset, the pyramids in the horizon. I was crying because I knew I would never return to this place, never again see the tree in the backyard perpetually laden with fat ripe mangoes, as orange as the Giza sunset, as sweet as my summers had been. My father, unaccustomed to my crying, told me that we would be back, but I knew he was just saying it to try to make me feel better.

That final evening, he made his specialty dish, the only thing he knew how to cook: steamed white rice with raw apples and bananas. I'd been eating it with him my entire short life, and as I stood there, watching the sunset, I knew my childhood was over. The more I ate, the less remained of the food, of him, and the more I looked out, the duller the sky grew, until the food was gone and the daylight was gone and my father's face became a silhouette, my childhood disappearing with it, digested quickly, between sobs. The following year, we moved to England and I never saw my father again.

I turned away from the mirror. The glorious days of my life as a stripper were ending. All that was left was to leave.

In the late fall, after much prodding from Ben, I finally met his parents. I stood in their lavish living room, among the hardwood everything that gleamed with a clean, lemon-scented twinkle. His mother resembled me somewhat, her hair dark and curly like mine, her figure somewhat petite. She greeted me with open arms, and I was immediately swept into her warm embrace. Ben's father was rugged, handsome, assured, and charming.

I helped his mother make coffee, and afterward we all sat and talked about nothing in particular as we sipped from sunny yellow teacups. They didn't grill me about my life, which was a relief. Ben had a wholesome relationship with his parents, and I watched their interaction with curiosity. They all looked so peaceful and were politely considerate of one another. Ben told his mother she looked pretty, and Ben's father called him "Son" and gave him hearty pats on the back as Ben smiled and said that he was so happy to see them. I thought of my own three-ring circus of a family, my mother screaming in the kitchen and throwing wooden spoons as my grandmother groaned and complained, the kids fighting, my stepfather walking around with that half-stunned look on his face, me off in my little corner, fuming as always.

During the drive home, Ben reassuringly told me that his parents liked me.

"Did you tell them I'm a stripper?" I asked.

"Sure," he said. "It's no big deal."

"You should've told me you told them," I said.

"Why? I didn't think you minded."

I didn't say anything.

"Does it bother you?" he asked. "I mean, they're really open and everything. It's no big deal, they're cool about it." It seemed like Ben had told his parents because he was proud of it himself.

"How can you be proud of what I do, yet so insecure about the lap dances?" I asked him. He looked startled.

"That's different," he said.

"How?" I pressed.

"I already told you," he responded, shifting in his seat uneasily.

We drove on in silence until he popped in a Radiohead CD and turned up the volume. When I turned down the volume, he stared at me.

"I thought you were getting uncomfortable with my dancing because you loved me," I said. "I didn't know you were proud of it."

"I do love you. I just don't like the lap dancing."

"But you're proud of the other dancing, right?"

He shrugged. "I don't know. I guess so, kind of."

I leaned back in my seat and opened the window, letting the wind rush into the car. "Why don't you just become my stripping manager?" I said into the wind.

"What?" He didn't hear me.

"Nothing. Never mind."

Then a strange thing began to happen to me at work. Instead of being reluctant to approach men, I suddenly found myself looking into their faces and eyes without feeling disgusted or detached. I now wanted to take care of them and make them feel that they could trust me. This shift was weird; it felt as if I were looking down on Layla from a high place, observing her while she spread her magic. I was losing myself and merging with a concept, the concept of Layla. As a person, I was fucked, but as a stripper, I had struck gold.

I started, quite suddenly, to understand the strippers I had once worked with, particularly the ones in the upscale clubs, with their charming and coy girlish ways. Maybe they weren't being fake, maybe they meant what they said, maybe they really cared about their customers.

The more I got into the men at the club, the more I shut out Ben, the same way I'd shut out Andrew. It was alarming how easy this was for me to do, and how much easier it was becoming every day. All the discomfort of compartmentalizing my life had ceased, as though I had finally found the shortcut to simplifying things, without the agony of trying to "get into character."

Now, "coming out of character" was my biggest problem. I was stuck in Layla mode, and when I left work, I grasped in vain at the threads of a former self I didn't know very well to begin with. If stripping were a mountain, I'd made it to the top, but I was now suffering altitude sickness. When I got home, Ben knocked at the exterior and was met with blank looks, or sudden tears of frustration.

"What's wrong with you?" he asked one night as I broke down crying. I couldn't answer him because I didn't know what was happening to me, but I knew that something was very wrong.

My Monday-night gig abruptly ended when I drove to Monaco Bob's one evening and found sheets of wood hastily nailed over the front door, sprayed over in neon orange letters that read OUT OF BIZNESS.

At the Lookie-Bar, I cultivated a way to make money outside of the club. It worked like this: I stood away from the other dancers and watched the men in the crowd. When I spotted one that looked sad and lonely, I approached and started a conversation, beginning with something superficial, such as the weather or the history of New Orleans. After a few minutes of warming them up, I probed deeper, asking about their jobs and their home lives. I didn't ask them to buy me a drink or pressure them for dances. I didn't do anything but listen to what they had to say or laugh at their jokes. I was, in fact, very interested. After all, these men were now people to me.

Eventually my questions grew more personal, about dreams and wishes and hopes. I talked about my life openly, as well. Then I told them that I wished they could spend time with me, somewhere else.

"I'm tired of being here anyway," I would say.

"Would you like to go have a drink?" they always asked, and I always said yes, I very much would like that. And I was not lying. I really was tired of the club, tired of the champagne-and-dance number, tired of the long hours I had to be there playing the same game, hoping it would all pay off at some point, though it never actually did.

Men were always thrown off at first when I told them that I didn't want them to buy me a drink in the club, but, rather, somewhere else. They had been trained to the club's rules of drink-buying and time-buying. But it was remarkably easy to undo that training; I was giving them a whiff of what they wanted, or thought they wanted: a chance to get to know the dancer outside the club's confines.

Once we were outside the club, I did not need to act a certain way and could be myself. I listened. I talked. I told jokes. All very ordinary, very casual. Except that I was being paid $250 to $500 for one to three hours of my "real self." Sometimes the conversations were very interesting. One high-paying customer and I got into an intense three-hour discussion about *A Confederacy of Dunces*, and another customer and I discussed ways to improve his marriage.

When it was time to go, I usually took their cards if they insisted on giving one to me (which, sadly, many did) and promised to call them, which was the only lie in the whole "scam." Sometimes they wanted me to give them my number, which I told them wasn't a good idea. I pulled this stunt about three times a week and worked one full shift a week so that no one at the club would notice what I was doing.

It wasn't always perfect, of course. Sometimes I got a man with expectations of more, like sex, or becoming a regular. But this was pretty rare. I mostly picked men who were from out of town, and they were easy to find in the French Quarter. It was like Phil all over again, without all the weird discomfort.

twenty-six

At Christmas, I junked my crappy car when my mother informed me my stepfather was sending his Toyota to me as a present. He had just bought himself a new sports car, so I was now the recipient of an actually reliable vehicle. As a result, Ben and I decided to take a road trip to Los Angeles.

It was the season of El Niño, and the weather got bad when we crossed the Texas border; by the time we were in New Mexico, we were driving through thick snow. Ben drove for the first part of the trip, and we fought a lot, as he was upset about my ignoring him and trying to write in the car, and I was going crazy from the blinding white of our surroundings. We finally pulled over to see Carlsbad Caverns, where I welcomed the cool darkness.

I took over the driving as we pushed on through the surreal backdrop of the Guadalupe Mountains, then headed north through another snowstorm. Ben was paranoid the whole time, trying to advise me on my driving while I tried to ignore him and watch the slick road with aching concentration. Eventually, he took out a camera and began neurotically taking pictures of the road, the interior of the car, of me yawning or yelling, and of the steering wheel and my hands clutching it.

We hit Sedona, Arizona, on Christmas Eve and celebrated it in a bed-and-breakfast nestled among monstrous red rocks. When we finally got to L.A., I chirped away excitedly as I pointed out my old hangouts. We stayed for a few days, and I found myself wanting to scrap everything to move back, go to school, and get a normal job.

"Would you consider moving here?" I asked Ben as we left Los Angeles for San Francisco.

He thought about it for a moment. "Hell, yeah. I could live here."

"Really?"

"Really."

Maybe life was going to turn out well after all. It was true that things between Ben and me hadn't been great lately, but maybe they'd get better once I quit dancing and began living an honest-to-God normal life. It seemed so simple, I thought to myself as we cruised the majestic coastline.

San Francisco was cold and sunny. Curious to see how things were at Gigi's, I ventured there one evening when Ben decided to go to bed early. The club looked the same from the outside, but when I walked inside I didn't see a familiar face until I ran into the manager, Sally. She hugged me and asked how I was doing, and told me that Divine was the only dancer left from the old group.

"She's back there, working," Sally said. "You can hang out and wait for her if you'd like."

I waited and watched, feeling oddly sentimental when I saw the red heart-shaped basket being passed around. The place looked so innocent and clean. When Divine emerged from the booths and saw me, she didn't look surprised in the least.

"I had a feeling you'd make your way back here," she said.

We headed up to the New Delhi for a drink, and I became highly irritated when I couldn't light up in the bar because of California's new no-smoking law.

Divine gave me the rundown on what had happened to the other girls over the past year and a half: Savannah got married and quit dancing altogether; Amber went to New York to dance; Haley went home to Texas and was supposedly going back to school; and Katiya had moved to Paris with her new boyfriend.

"Boyfriend?" I asked, astonished.

Divine waved a dismissive hand. "Please, did you ever believe the dyke thing with her? She just stopped screwing guys for a while and needed to justify it."

I asked Divine if she had plans to stop dancing anytime soon. She'd been doing it for eight years.

"Every year I go through this thing where I say to myself, 'That's it, this year I'm going to quit.' But then the mood passes, and I have so much money put away. I'm thinking of retiring in five years or so, after paying off my place, maybe doing some traveling, I don't know."

"You know," she continued, "most people work a nine-to-five job for, what, twenty-five, thirty years? Then they retire. Stripping for eight years feels like twenty, so in five years, I figure it will all be evened out."

She asked if I was still dancing, and I gave her the rundown of what I was doing in New Orleans. When I mentioned my newest money-making scheme that involved having drinks with customers at a nearby bar, she cracked up.

"So you say you want to quit, but now you're dragging the club with you into the outside world." While this was kind of funny, it was also kind of pathetic.

"You were always too nice," she pointed out. "That was your biggest problem."

"I'm not too nice anymore."

"Well," she said, "that's probably because all the goddamn niceness is getting sapped out of you. You're too pretty on the inside to do this kind of work."

"I'm not so pretty."

"No, I mean you're sensitive, too sensitive to it. You aren't ruthless enough."

"But I want to be ruthless," I complained.

"Well, you aren't," she said bluntly. "That might not be such a bad thing, you know. I don't know why you think you have to be that way. What are you trying to prove to yourself anyway?"

"I have no idea," I said. "But I don't think I can do it anymore."

"Then you should stop," she stated simply. "This isn't a job just anyone can do. It gets to everyone. But it gets to some more than others, and if it is getting to you, then you should stop before you become even more of a jaded bitch." She checked her watch. "Shit, Layla, I have to get back, I've got a set." Then she suddenly looked around, quite annoyed. "You know, this no-smoking thing is a fucking joke."

We walked back, and when we reached the club, something dawned on me.

"Divine," I asked, "what's your real name?" I always found it strange how in my years of dancing I had had intimate and in-depth conversations with these women, had been naked with them, yet had never learned their real names.

"It's Amy. God, I am so not an Amy," she laughed.

Amy and I hugged, then she went into the club. I never saw her again.

When I got back to New Orleans, the sights, smells, and sounds of stripping suddenly ganged up on me all at once. Things that had always been there, the accumulated little elements that had never disturbed me before, were now driving me crazy. The fluorescent lights that shone down on the ratty, torn, brown fake-leather seats. The lipstick smears on the mirror. The chalky, sweet smells of fruit sprays, cigarettes, cheap deodorant, and disinfectant. Cough drops and vapor rub. Broken powder compacts. Ashtrays caked with ancient ashes. Torn costumes slung over broken chairs. Cheap glitter on the frayed carpet. Old gray and neon bubble gum stuck to the counter. A Polaroid of someone's inner thigh. Brushes caked with dried hair spray and dandruff. Toenail clippers and eyelash curlers, nail-polish stains on the wall, EAT ME written in blood-red nail polish, splinters and stale spilled champagne and rotting wood and ... all of it!

One night, I noticed a new dancer with dyed black hair, love handles, and oily skin avidly sucking champagne from a glass through a fat straw. With a free hand, she fondled the thigh of her customer, a young clean-cut guy. He kissed her plump manicured hand, and I tried not to gawk when she lunged over and kissed him on the lips, her mouth open, revealing their tongues doing a sword dance. I looked around to see if anyone noticed. No one cared. They untangled for a moment, breathing and nuzzling. Feeling eyes on her, she looked over at me and smiled and winked, red lipstick smeared around the edges of her mouth, down to her chin. I smiled back because it was the thing to do, then watched as she got up to dance a set.

Onstage she strutted in a white spandex dress, her spiky black heels and skinny ankles gripping the pole as she twirled around it. A gold anklet glistened as she wiggled over to her customer, who sat at the foot of the stage, a dumb smile on his lips as he leaned over, looked up at her, and threw down some small bills.

When I was twelve, I read an article in one of those annoying women's magazines for bored housewives about seducing your significant other by stripping for him. As I read the article, I pictured in my head a mousy woman seated in a cubicle at work. Things were not too passionate these days between her and her husband, so she thought about spicing things up with a little dancing. As I sat and watched the black stilettos of this woman move across the stage, I was taken back to that article. The entire scene reeked of "Surprise Him Tonight!" and for some reason that was the final straw. I walked out at the end of my shift and never went back.

I'd thought that quitting stripping would be good for my relationship with Ben, but a week after I walked out of the Lookie-Bar, we broke up.

It all happened in Nashville, where we'd gone for a little getaway. One night in the hotel, as we were getting ready for bed, he blurted out unceremoniously that he thought we should date other people. I stood around in shock as he cried. I threw my clothes in my suitcase to leave, then pulled them out and threw them at him.

"I don't want to break up with you," he cried, but then he told me that he didn't love me, wasn't sure he ever did. Then he swung the other way and told me that he did love me but wasn't sure how to love. Then he told that me he thought he wanted other women and was "curious about their pussies." He told me that last statement as he was backing away from me in fear, even though I hadn't reacted at all.

This went on for hours, his every word and decision and indecision leaving me dangling helplessly. I began to wonder if Ben was just crazy, his wholesome upbringing nothing but a tidy window display that didn't remotely match the horrific merchandise inside the shop.

Even if we stayed together, Ben said, I should know that an old female friend that he used to date was coming into town and staying with him. He suggested that he and I not see each other the week she was visiting. Ben said this in a scared voice, and his fear was like a hint of blood in the air, which I ruthlessly chased after.

"You want to get laid that week, so you want to take a time-out from the relationship so that there's no guilt for you to deal with?"

"No, it isn't like that," he tried to argue. "I know it looks suspicious—"

"No, Ben," I interrupted. "It is not suspicious. It is goddamn pathetic. I mean, you could work a little harder to hide your motives. It would make the sex with her more exciting.

"And speaking of sex," I ranted. "What the fuck do you have to complain about? There isn't a fantasy you've not had granted from me, you asshole."

"It's not about sex!" he cried. "I don't want to have sex with her, it isn't like that. I just want to use that week to think about our relationship. That's why I need the time apart."

"You are a lying sack of shit," I said, getting up to go to the bathroom. When I returned, he was crying.

"What the hell are you crying about?" I screamed, which made him cry harder.

"It's too hard to do this," he said. "Talking to you is. . . . It makes me feel impotent sometimes."

"Impotent? Where does your dick figure into this drama?" I yelled. "You had ten inches added to you since you met me, and now you're losing your imaginary hard-on and that's the most important thing?"

Ben was so scared of my anger, my pain, and all the things that I had kept locked inside me. He never raised his voice to me, always avoided arguments because he knew I could not only rationalize everything but also bully him into seeing things my way. He always walked a delicate path around me, afraid to speak his mind and risk setting me off, and I in turn hated myself for being so unapproachable and hated him for not seeing past all of it.

When we returned to New Orleans, I dropped him off, ignoring his words, ignoring him. It was over. Then, for some reason, I turned around and drove right back to Nashville. I needed not to think about thinking, and driving was perfect for that.

I drove all night, an endless stream of cigarette smoke propelling me through the grimy darkness. When I arrived back in Nashville, I checked into a motel downtown, and the clerk, an old woman with a puff of white hair, eyed me suspiciously, as I probably looked like a crackhead, my sleepless eyes glassy and sunken in my unwashed head.

Something about motels and hotels had always soothed me. Here was this place that was mine, but with no attachment; I didn't have to worry about maintaining it or having it resurrect any memories. Most rooms looked alike; they didn't pose danger with promises of sentimentality or nostalgia. It was just the bare necessities, a place where people came when they were weary or horny.

I spent the next three days either lying in bed watching television in my motel room or driving to get food to bring back and eat in bed while watching television in my motel room. Eventually, I ventured out to explore Nashville. The ASCAP (American Society of Composers, Authors, and Publishers) convention was in town, and all kinds of music producers were around, trying to find the next hot thing in country music. I hit a few clubs to hear some live music and got a kick out of musicians asking me if I was affiliated with a record label. In a crazy moment—there were a lot of those—I considered moving to Nashville and starting from scratch. But I was tired of starting from scratch. I was tired of everything.

Later that week, I went to the movies to see *As Good As It Gets*. As I was settling down with a tub of popcorn, the power suddenly went off. A few minutes later, an usher hurried in, flashlight in hand, and announced in a stony, controlled voice that a tornado was hitting the city.

Everyone scrambled out to the parking lot, bewildered. I got into my car, completely clueless about tornadoes, except for the understanding that I didn't want to be caught in one. I tried following the traffic until I got caught in a terrible jam. Scared out of my wits, I turned around and headed down a less congested street. I looked up at the yellowish sky and saw an ominous swirling pattern beginning to gather far off in the distance. I turned around again, driving down another street that led nowhere. Finally, I calmed down, figured out where I was going, and found my way back to my motel.

"We have to evacuate!" the clerk screamed.

I gathered my things from my room, then got back in my car and starting driving again. A voice on the radio announced that the tornado was about to hit downtown. I freaked out and stopped into a gas station. The attendant was running around frantically. I asked him what I should do.

"Get out of Nashville," he said. "Go to East Nashville, that's where we're all going."

I headed east and eventually checked into a room at the Holiday Inn in East Nashville. I turned on the TV and saw footage of a few downtown buildings with their roofs blown off. I called my mother.

"Jesus!" she screamed into the phone. "What the hell are you doing in Nashville?"

"Calm down," I said. "I'm in East Nashville. It's where people were evacuated to."

"Are you nuts?" my mother hollered. "You don't know what's going to happen, you'll die, come back to Florida, come here now!" Then she started rattling on about the car. Was it okay? If I got caught in the tornado, it would be destroyed. My mother was an intelligent woman, but her mind moved so fast that words often fell out of her mouth with no logic attached to them, which made her sound like a complete airhead.

I eventually hung up on her and reluctantly called Ben. He was hysterical when he found out where I was, and it made me pitifully happy that he cared. I fell asleep as he talked, then woke up later with the phone receiver still cradled next to my head. The next morning I started back for New Orleans, my mind oddly calm. It was a startlingly clear, sunny day with no traces of tornado terror.

However, a few hours after I entered Mississippi, the grayish-yellow sky slowly returned. Then an odd, slight swirling pattern appeared in the sky. I drove faster, not knowing what else to do. Was it possible to be followed by a tornado? I babbled prayers to myself and turned on the radio, from which I heard about a tornado warning in Lamar County. Two miles later, I passed a sign that said LAMAR COUNTY.

The sky went dark, even though it was three in the afternoon. In the distance I saw some trees lying in the road. I slowed down and carefully drove onto the median to get past the damage. What the hell was I supposed to do? Was I supposed to pull over? Was I supposed to turn around? Another car quickly sped ahead of me. I expected to be carried off into the funnel, then spat out somewhere, maybe onto Ben's doorstep, what was left of the car mangled and bent, a steering wheel, a lock of hair, a severed hand, white-knuckled, clutching a cigarette filter, ashes everywhere.

It didn't come to that. I somehow missed the tornado, or it missed me. Miraculously, the sky brightened a few moments later, and I drove straight through to New Orleans without further incident.

When I got to Ben's place, he answered the door, his face unshaven and pale, his hair unwashed. He embraced me, and I fell into his arms.

Later that evening, my heart vibrated as we went through the ritual of preparing for bed, knowing it was the last time I would be doing so with Ben. In the dark, we held each other quietly, listening to each other's body, trying to see if the natural rhythm of our relationship had returned. It hadn't.

In a last desperate attempt, we groped around in the darkness, then had sex. Nothing. We were breaking up, not making up; our bodies didn't change temperature, didn't move with that slow, bittersweet ache that made hesitation melt. Instead, we made love like self-conscious strangers. So much for the lurid hunger that bound two people together and made their bodies understand something that their minds couldn't grasp.

I woke up alone the next morning, the covers tangled around my body after a fitful sleep. I got out of bed and headed down to the kitchen, where Ben stood, looking like he had been waiting for me.

"Rania—" he started to say, but I didn't want to hear his speech.

"I'm moving back to Los Angeles," I said.

He stood over the kitchen sink, holding a sponge, wringing then releasing over and over again. "I don't want you to go," he finally said, "but I can't go with you."

"You're absolutely sure?" I asked, and he nodded, his eyes gathering tears.

"Maybe later," he said. "But not now." Then he walked over to the corner wall and sunk into it, as if wanting to be embraced by the creamy thickness of each layer of paint.

I went home and cried for three straight days. Just as I thought I was done crying, it would start again. My roommate timidly knocked on my door, and I told her I was fine. Eventually I passed out in exhaustion and slept for a day. On the fourth day, I got up, washed my face, ate, packed my bags and boxes, and paid off my

rent for the following month. Then I got in my car and drove to
Los Angeles.

twenty-seven

During the summers of my childhood, my grandmother and I used to visit her older brother. He was a retired architect, and when he was younger, he'd married an English woman and designed a large house for her overlooking the pyramids of Giza. In the late afternoons, I would sit beneath an Indian mango tree in the garden, eating a recently fallen, sticky, ripe mango, licking its juice off my fingers, as I waited for my father to pick me up.

Once my father got me, we would drive through the ruins and temples of Giza toward his house as he blasted *baladi*–Egyptian folk music. We maneuvered along the narrow winding roads, the car speakers booming with tribal drumming, hypnotic chanting, and the loud clinking of cymbals. The sunset resembled an ignited flame. I would join in as my father howled at the top of his lungs to the music. In my memory, the earth howled back in reply. When I remember my first taste of wild, uninhibited freedom, I recall those drives with my father.

I thought about that feeling often during my first six months back in L.A. For money, I did temp work–mundane jobs like answering phones and filing, anything to make ends meet. A lot of times I couldn't make ends meet and had to ask my family for help, which they didn't like. Dancing had spoiled me financially; it wasn't how great the money had been, it was how quickly I could get my hands on it. For three years, all I had to do was work an extra shift whenever I was a few hundred dollars short. Now I had to work an extra two weeks, and the bills had to get an extension from the extension.

I often had dreams about dancing. Some were anxiety-driven—I was due onstage immediately for my set, but some part of my costume was missing, like my shoes. But one strange dream was recurrent: It was the scene from the movie *Gone with the Wind* when Scarlett is walking among the injured Confederate soldiers. Slowly the camera slowly pans out, revealing an entire field of men crying and moaning for help. In my dream, the men were lying with erect penises, awaiting lap dances from me. I always woke up laughing, then began crying hysterically a few seconds later.

I still missed the stage, the adrenaline of being up there, silent and naked, that breathtaking, sudden, initial realization of freedom. One night I packed my dancing clothes and drove to a strip club. I sat outside in my car, trying to decide whether to go in, the music thumping into the street as a stream of men entered the club, then stumbled out. A young, muscle-bound man was stationed at the front door, fiddling with what looked to be a Game Boy. The entire scene looked so sadly ordinary. I sat there forever, wondering what to do, wondering what the draw had once been.

I didn't go inside.